DANGER IN THE SNOW

ALASKA COZY MYSTERY #9

WENDY MEADOWS

Copyright © 2019 by Wendy Meadows

All rights reserved.

No part of this publication may be reproduced, distributed or transmitted in any form or by any means, without prior written permission.

This is a work of fiction. Names, characters, places, and incidents are a product of the author's imagination. Locales and public names are sometimes used for atmospheric purposes. Any resemblance to actual people, living or dead, or to businesses, companies, events, institutions, or locales is completely coincidental.

CHAPTER ONE

Sarah walked into the kitchen of her cozy, warm cabin wearing a pink bathrobe that she had purchased at O'Mally's. The bathrobe was new and so fluffy it made even the cold morning feel inviting. "Ah," she sighed happily as she poured herself a cup of coffee, "an entire morning to myself. Maybe I can finally get caught up on my work." Sarah glanced out the kitchen window and studied the snowstorm just beginning to howl through the trees outside. "Maybe I'll soak in a hot bath later and warm my bones," she added.

Mittens, Sarah's Husky puppy, let out a little whine and looked at the back door. Sarah let out a low moan. "Oh no, not again," she begged. "Conrad let you out before he left for work." Mittens sat up on the brown corduroy dog bed resting in the warmest corner of the kitchen and trotted over to the back door. "Oh...poor thing," Sarah sighed and let out a laugh. "Okay...okay, I'll go get dressed. Give me a few minutes."

Sarah put down her coffee and left the kitchen. She returned ten minutes later dressed for the freezing weather and donned a heavy parka over her burgundy wool dress. "Just a second," she told Mittens and quickly pulled on a pair of white gloves and a warm pink ski hat. "Okay...boots...hat...gloves...coat...we're all set, girl," she smiled and opened the back door. "Let's go." Mittens let out a happy bark and stormed out into the snow. Sarah wrapped her arms together, eased out into an icy wind, glanced up at the heavy falling snow, and closed the back door behind them. "Wait up," she called out and hurried around to the back of the cabin after Mittens.

As Mittens searched the snow around her favorite trees, a truck rumbled past on the front road. Sarah spotted the truck. A broad smile appeared across her face. "June Bug is home, Mittens. She's back from London. Come on!" Mittens quickly finished her business under the trees and ran after Sarah.

"June Bug!" Sarah called out and began waving her hands as Amanda pulled her truck into the driveway.

Amanda, who was usually the sort to honk the horn like crazy, eased her truck to a stop behind Sarah's jeep, put it in park, and sat very silent. Sarah stopped waving, stared at the truck, and then hurried over to the driver's side door and opened it. "June Bug?" she asked. Sensing that something was terribly wrong, Sarah took her gloved hand and lifted Amanda's chin. Amanda's eyes were full of tears. "Oh honey, what's the matter?"

"It's...it's too horrible..." Amanda whimpered and wiped at her nose.

"Did something happen? Are you okay? Is your husband okay?" Sarah asked.

Amanda shook her head no. "I'm fine—my hubby is fine. But he...he had to stay behind in London. Again. But that's not it..." Amanda lowered her eyes and let out a painful moan.

"And your son—?"

"My son is in London with my hubby," Amanda explained as frosty snow began to stick to her face. She grabbed a green ski cap and held it down on her head with her white glove.

"Then what's the matter? Did you and your husband have a fight?" Sarah asked, confused.

"Oh no...we're still warm in each other's hearts," Amanda assured Sarah.

Sarah wiped the heavy falling snow away from her face and hugged her arms and tucked her chin down against the wind. "Did someone pass away?" she guessed, at a loss.

Amanda shook her head no. "Everyone is alive and well."

Sarah felt increasingly confused. "Then why are you crying, honey?" she begged. Mittens propped her paws against the open car door, looking at Sarah and waiting for Amanda to answer.

Amanda lifted her teary eyes up to Sarah and tried to speak again, but began sobbing before she could say anything much. "Oh, it's too horrible!"

Sarah looked down at Mittens, shrugged her shoulders, and then focused on the snow soaking her cold face. "Honey, you're going to freeze. Come inside where it's warm."

"I can't...it feels like the world is about to come to an end. How can I possibly go inside and warm my...my tortured heart?" Amanda cried. "I would rather sit here and freeze into an iceberg."

Sarah pressed her lips together and tried to understand what could possibly be making her best friend so upset. "Did you...ruin a new dress?" she asked, grasping at straws. She quickly snatched onto an idea. "Oh, maybe that's it. Did the airport lose your luggage and all the new dresses you bought in London? Oh honey, I'm so sorry."

"No, no. Don't worry about that. All of the dresses I purchased are safely at home," Amanda promised through a quiet, sobbing wail.

"Then honey, what's the matter?" Sarah asked as her teeth began chattering together.

Amanda's face twisted into a painful expression. The poor woman looked as if someone were taking a wrench and pulling her teeth out. "Bertha," she hissed.

"Bertha?" Sarah asked. "Who is Bertha?"

Amanda grabbed Sarah's hands as if she were about to fall off a cliff. "She's...oh, words can't describe her," she exclaimed with wide, terrified eyes.

"Honey, you better come inside with me." Sarah pulled Amanda out of the truck and hurried her back inside. "Now," she said, taking off the brown coat Amanda was wearing and hanging it on the wooden coat rack next to the back door, "go sit down and I'll pour you a cup of coffee."

Mittens scampered in behind Amanda, then walked over to her dog bed and lay down. Now that Amanda's coat was off, it was apparent she was wearing a strange—if not crazy—blue dress with colorful flowers on it. Sarah did not comment, worried about her friend's mental state. Amanda let out a heavy moan, clomped over the kitchen table, and plopped down like a woman whose life was coming to an end. "Make my coffee black, Los Angeles."

Sarah closed the back door, hung up her coat, and hurried to pour Amanda a cup of coffee. "Now honey, take a deep breath, try to calm down, and tell me: who is this Bertha person?"

Amanda lifted her eyes. "She's too horrible to speak of," she whispered.

Sarah sighed, walked a cup of coffee over to the kitchen table, and sat down. "Here, take your coffee," she told Amanda.

"Oh, how the warm flavors of coffee once caressed my sad lips," Amanda sighed. "Never again will the sweet taste of java warm this weary, torn heart."

Sarah put her hand over her face and fought back laughter. Amanda shot her a serious look. "Sorry," Sarah apologized, "but you're being so...dramatic."

"Dramatic?" Amanda asked as fresh tears flooded down her cheeks, "Do these tears look...dramatic to you?"

Sarah shot Mittens a desperate look. Mittens tucked her head between her paws. "Uh...well...I'm just a little...confused," Sarah eased forward like she was walking on eggshells. "You turn up looking like someone killed your loved ones, you won't answer my questions except to tell me nothing is wrong except for this mysterious Bertha person. Why don't you start there and explain why she's so awful? Who is she?"

"Who is she?" Amanda asked in a hysterical voice, "Who is she? I'll tell you who she is..." Amanda grimaced, holding back tears. "She's my...nanny," she whimpered.

"Your nanny?" Sarah asked. Amanda bowed her head. "Honey, aren't you a bit too old for a nanny?"

"Not according to my hubby," Amanda replied in a pained voice. "I've been getting into so much trouble lately that my hubby..." Amanda squeezed her eyes closed. "My husband had to stay in London so he hired my old nanny to fly to Alaska and babysit me. She'll be in town tomorrow morning...she's already in Fairbanks. Oh..." she groaned and hid her face again.

Sarah grinned, finding the whole thing suddenly quite humorous. "Bertha is...your old nanny?"

Amanda popped her eyes open. "Not funny, love," she fussed. "Bertha is...a nightmare." Amanda grabbed her coffee, took a sip, and burned her tongue in the process. "Oh drat," she complained.

"June Bug, calm down," Sarah pleaded, fighting back laughter. "I'm sure that your gracious husband meant well."

"Oh, I know he meant well," Amanda whined, "and I'm not angry at him. After all, he's not wrong. You and I did come close to dying...on more than one occasion." Amanda set down her coffee and checked her burned tongue. "You see," she explained, "Bertha hates me. She loathes the very air I breathe. Of course, in the eyes of other people she pretends to worship the ground I walk on…but in private," Amanda shivered all over, "she turns into a hideous monster."

"Honey," Sarah said, "you're a grown woman. If you don't like this woman, send her packing. This is a free country. No one should ever be subjected to such cruel and unusual…treatment," Sarah finished and covered a grin with her right hand as quickly as possible.

"Not funny, Los Angeles," Amanda griped. "I'm sinking in quicksand and you're making fun." Amanda shook her head. "Shame on you…shame, shame, shame."

"Sorry, June Bug," Sarah apologized, fighting back laughter, "it's just that…well, honey, you're a grown woman. I can understand if you were a child in a fairytale, but you're…you're not even close to twenty anymore."

"I know," Amanda replied and then let out a miserable cry. "And Bertha has aged into something worse…an old, bitter, hateful monster." Amanda looked at Sarah with desperate eyes. "She's even worse now than when I was a young girl…oh, far, far worse. And now…Bertha is on her way to our town." Amanda bolted to her feet, ran to the pantry, and locked herself inside.

"June Bug," Sarah said and rolled her eyes, "hiding in my pantry isn't the answer."

"Maybe Bertha won't find me in here," Amanda called

out from the pantry. Mittens raised her head, stared at the pantry door, and then went back to sleep.

"What a morning," Sarah sighed and stood up. She walked over to the pantry door and knocked. "Anyone home?"

"Just us scared chickens."

"Well Mrs. Scared Chicken, can I lure you out of hiding long enough to eat a cinnamon roll? I baked them last night."

Silence fell in the kitchen. Only the sound of the winter winds spoke. And then Amanda's voice whispered, "Cinnamon rolls? Fresh ones?"

"Baked a batch last night," Sarah promised.

"Did you add the special frosting I like?"

"I sure did," Sarah smiled.

Silence fell again. Amanda considered the offer Sarah had placed in her lap. "Stay safe in the pantry...or cinnamon rolls?" she whispered. After a few seconds she made her decision. "Maybe...just one," she told Sarah as she crept out of the pantry with sad, puppy-dog eyes.

"Oh, June Bug," Sarah laughed. She wrapped her arms around Amanda and walked her back to the kitchen table. "I'll get you a cinnamon roll." Sarah walked to the refrigerator and retrieved Amanda a cinnamon roll, placed it on a green plate, and heated it up in the microwave. When it beeped, she took it out and made her way back to the kitchen table. "Here, honey."

Amanda sighed. She looked toward the kitchen window. "Maybe she'll run off the road into the snow and turn up missing?"

"June Bug," Sarah scolded Amanda in a playful voice, "that's a horrible thing to say."

"I...suppose," Amanda agreed. She gently picked up her cinnamon roll and took a bite. "Los Angeles, if I could only put into words how awful Bertha is. You're the writer. I wish I had your gift for words."

"Try, June Bug," Sarah urged Amanda.

Amanda kept her eyes on the kitchen window. "When I was a young girl Bertha used to...what's a good word...oh yes...torture me."

"Torture?" Sarah asked. She leaned across the table, picked up Amanda's coffee, and took a sip. "Torture is a very strong word."

"Torture is the correct word," Amanda promised Sarah. She finally looked away from the cinnamon bun. "Bertha tortured me in...how should I put this...oh, let's say...non-physical ways."

"You mean mentally and emotionally?"

"Yes, that's exactly right," Amanda agreed. "Bertha was...vicious with her words and actions, even if she never left a mark on me. All carried out behind closed doors, far from my parents' eyes and ears, of course. Bertha presented herself as the perfect nanny to the public eye. Oh, my parents simply adored her...that monster."

Sarah began to feel the seriousness of Amanda's desperation. The situation no longer seemed amusing or funny. "Talk to me, June Bug."

Amanda looked Sarah straight in the eyes. "My parents gave Bertha full authority over me," she said in a tragic voice. "Bertha would...make up lies...horrible, vicious lies...and tell things to my parents. She would never say a kind word to me...simply smile that evil, cold smile...and behind my back she was working to destroy my life. I...I tried to tell my parents the truth, but they thought I was just being a willful child, trying to get a competent, innocent woman terminated from her position simply because I didn't like her style of discipline. I always was a spirited child and I think they were grateful that Bertha was able to manage me so expertly. They had no idea how she did it...oh, if only they knew the truth. Bertha was a permanent fixture in our home until I grew old enough to truly defend myself against her. Then one day my mother caught her in a lie...after years of agony...and she sent Bertha packing, as you Americans say."

"Why didn't you tell me about this woman?" Sarah asked.

"Because I blocked her from my memory," Amanda confessed. "Why would I ever think about her? I assumed I would never see her again. But...oh, Los Angeles, she's working as a home nurse now. When my hubby and I arrived in London we had to visit an agency and arrange for my father-in-law to have a home nurse...and guess...oh, guess who was at the agency?"

"Bertha?"

"Yes, evil smile and all." Amanda shivered all over. "And oh, Los Angeles, she pulled my dear hubby into her sticky web quicker than he could blink. I didn't even see it happen."

"What did she do?"

"I didn't know until later...while we were there, I stood politely by, waited for my hubby to arrange to hire the home nurse, and we left. I thought...well, that was the end of that horrible experience. But when I arrived in Alaska last night, my husband called me and told me he also hired Bertha to be a...what was his words...oh yes, a Personal Sitter for me, someone to watch me and keep me from trouble while he's away."

"June Bug, just call your husband and tell him the truth."

"I did," Amanda replied in misery. "I told him right then and there. He wouldn't be moved. He said I was being childish, and anyway he already paid Bertha's salary for one full month...and well, when my hubby spends a penny he expects his money's worth."

"Yeah...your husband is—"

"Cheap," Amanda finished for Sarah.

"Afraid so."

Amanda sighed. "Bertha is coming to extract her revenge, Los Angeles. She's coming to finish me off for getting her dismissed from her position." Amanda looked at Sarah. "Love, can I stay with you? Please and pretty please with sugar on top, and all the sweets you can imagine."

"You know my home is your home," Sarah assured Amanda. "And with Conrad around, perhaps this woman will keep on the right side of the law."

Amanda shook her head. "Keep Conrad away from her," she begged Sarah. "Bertha will wrap Conrad around her little finger and have him eating out of her hand."

"Is this woman really that awful?"

"Evil is the word," Amanda confirmed.

Sarah looked toward the kitchen window. "June Bug, I trust you with my life and if you say this Bertha woman is evil then I believe you. I'll warn Conrad. In the meantime, we better drive to your house and pack a suitcase."

"Already did, love. My suitcase is in the truck." Amanda picked up her cinnamon roll. "My hubby insisted I let Bertha be a sitter for me...he didn't say I had to sleep in the same cabin with her. As long as I keep my distance and only entertain her when you're around...I should be okay."

Sarah shifted her eyes to Amanda. A very bad feeling settled in her stomach.

Conrad grinned at Amanda. It wasn't that he thought her situation was funny. It was...well, he thought to himself standing beside the fireplace in the living room, typical Amanda. A little over-dramatic, to say the least. "How old is Bertha?" he asked, stoking the fire with a fire iron.

"Seventy...maybe older, maybe younger, but somewhere around there," Amanda told Conrad and pointed a harsh finger at him. "Not a word from you, Conrad Spencer, do you hear me?"

Conrad grinned again and decided to tease Amanda a little. "Hey, I've tangled with my share of vicious street thugs back in New York. I've even run into purse-packing old ladies who gave me a run for my money. Scary stuff."

Amanda stuck her tongue out at Conrad. "You're a bloody riot. Not funny, Conrad."

DANGER IN THE SNOW

Sarah walked into the living room carrying a wooden tray with coffee cups and a carafe. "How are things going in here?" she asked in a careful voice. "Did you tell him?"

"He's making fun of me," Amanda complained.

"Is he?" Sarah asked and gave Conrad a look that said *Please, not tonight*.

Conrad smiled. "Okay," he whispered and continued to stoke the fire as the snowstorm raging outside howled and screamed. Conrad didn't mind the storm. The living room was warm, toasty and cozy. The warmth of the living room fought off the dangerous, icy fingers of the night, allowing Conrad to enjoy the snowstorm from a safe haven.

"Here, honey," Sarah said and handed Amanda a coffee.

"Thanks, love," Amanda sighed.

Sarah handed a coffee to Conrad and gazed into the fire. It crackled and leapt with warmth in the fireplace. "The fire is lovely," she said and hugged Conrad's arm. "I love nights like this...snow storms...warm fires...hot coffee...a writer's dream."

Conrad looked into Sarah's eyes, found his home, kissed the tip of her nose, and smiled. "You can shovel my truck out tomorrow morning," he teased.

"Oh, I'll leave that to you," Sarah laughed. She sat down on the couch. "Now," she said in a relaxed voice, "I'm hoping this snowstorm will prevent anyone from traveling into Snow Falls anytime soon. Our town is safe for the night."

Conrad agreed. He put down the fire iron, placed his coffee on the mantle of the fireplace, and removed his black leather jacket. "This storm is forecasted to dig itself in for a while," he said.

Amanda watched Conrad hang his leather jacket on a wooden coat rack next to the front door. She liked the leather jacket but didn't care so much for the gray sweater he wore under it, which Sarah had knitted for him; Conrad didn't care so much for the sweater himself, but what could a husband say or do when his wife presents him with a gift she slaved over? "Just you wait. Bertha will find a way into Snow Falls...that woman hates me," she said in a miserable voice.

Conrad walked back to the fireplace, took his coffee, eased over to a comfortable brown sitting chair that he insisted (well, begged) Sarah to let him have, and sat down. "Amanda, is this old lady truly as bad as you're making her out to be?" he asked.

"Yes," Amanda said. She took a sip of coffee and then eyed a plate of freshly baked brownies on the coffee table. "Why not?" she asked herself and snatched up a brownie. "I might as well die fat and happy."

"Oh honey," Sarah said, "you're not going to die. No one

is going to hurt you. Conrad and I are going to guard you every second Bertha is in town."

Amanda shifted her eyes to Conrad. "Bertha will have this poor bloke eating out of her hand in a matter of minutes," she promised Sarah.

Sarah looked at Conrad. Conrad shrugged his shoulders. "I'm a sap?" he asked.

"Not a sap...a man," Amanda sighed. "There isn't a man alive who can resist Bertha's...charm." Amanda nibbled on her brownie. "Bertha can sweet-talk a grizzly bear into giving up a freshly caught fish."

Sarah sipped at her coffee. She believed every word her best friend said but didn't want to spend the night fretting over someone who was being kept at bay by a powerful snowstorm. Sarah knew she would deal with Bertha when the old woman arrived, and until then, she simply wanted to enjoy the night with her husband and dearest friend. But, she thought, because Amanda was her dearest friend, Sarah didn't want to diminish any kind of worry that needed to be discussed. "June Bug, are you certain this woman is traveling to Snow Falls to harm you?"

Conrad leaned forward and took a brownie. "It's been many years since you've last seen this Bertha lady," he told Amanda. "Why would she wait all these years to harm you?"

"Because Bertha had no idea where I was living," Amanda confessed. "After I left my parents' home and went off to school, she couldn't find me." Amanda stared at her brownie and then looked around the warm living room. "Back in those days you didn't have the internet," she continued. "Today you can track anyone down just using their name. But in those days, things were different, especially in London. I kept my name unlisted in the phonebooks and directories and made sure I was never mentioned in the local newspapers or university publications. Bertha couldn't simply type my name into a search engine and track me down like a hound scenting a fox."

"Things sure were different in those days," Sarah agreed.

"Better," Amanda sighed. "Not that it stopped crimes completely. Cruel people determined to harm others will always find a way to do it. But at least you could avoid the public eye if you wanted to." Amanda looked toward the fireplace and studied the fire. She listened to the fire crackling as it burned the heavy logs Conrad had brought in from outside. The scent of the steady fire cast a gentle, warm feeling around the living room that calmed the worried heart. "When I married and took my husband's last name, I felt sure that Bertha would never be able to locate me. Besides," Amanda explained, "my mother told me Bertha had left London and moved into the country."

"And you never saw her again?" Conrad asked.

"Not once," Amanda replied. "Not until my husband and I walked into that home nurse agency."

Conrad took a bite of brownie. "Amanda, are you sure you're not overreacting?" he asked. "It seems excessive for her to exact revenge over being fired from a nanny job so many decades ago. It's not as if she never found a job again – obviously she's doing fine."

"No," Amanda said in a stern voice. "Conrad, I'm not some hysterical schoolgirl worrying about an old teacher threatening to smack my hand with a ruler."

Sarah read something in Amanda's eyes that worried her. "June Bug, is there something you're keeping from us?"

Amanda grew silent. She kept her eyes on the fire. After a couple of moments passed, she said, "Bertha threatened to kill me."

"Kill you?" Sarah asked.

Amanda rubbed her wrist. "The day my mother dismissed her and told her to leave our home, Bertha went to her room and began packing. She spotted me watching her from the upstairs hallway...I had snuck up there alone. Mother was downstairs in the living room waiting for her." Amanda raised her eyes and looked at Sarah. "Bertha's face twisted into an evil look...the look of a true monster. On her way downstairs, she leaned forward and whispered into my ear the words...the words..."

"What?" Sarah asked.

"'Someday I will return and punish you.'"

Conrad glanced at Sarah and then looked at Amanda. "Amanda, did Bertha say she would actually try to harm you?"

"I just told you what she—"

"You said Bertha promised to punish you," Conrad pointed out. "That could mean anything from a slap on the behind to no dessert for a week. Those words, even spoken with malice years ago, wouldn't hold up in a court of law."

"I'm afraid Conrad is right," Sarah agreed.

"I know, I know," Amanda said in despair. "That's the worst part. Bertha is clever...she would never put herself in a situation where she could be held responsible." Amanda closed her eyes. "The way she spoke those awful words...there was murder in her voice."

"And you believe this woman is coming here to fulfill that old promise?" Conrad asked.

"What, do you have ears full of wax? Haven't you been listening to me?" Amanda exploded at Conrad. Then she sighed. "I'm sorry. Thinking back to all of this makes me so upset. I didn't mean to shout at you like a child."

Sarah sipped at her coffee and listened to the winds

rushing through the pine forest outside. "June Bug, when Bertha arrives, I'm going to send her away. I know your husband will complain, but I'll explain the situation to him when he returns home. There's no sense in your being upset like this."

"He will be furious with me," Amanda worried. "The money..."

"I'll pay him back the money he spent on Bertha," Sarah assured Amanda and patted her hand. "He'll come out even-steven. I'll even pay to fly Bertha back to London."

"That's a good idea and the simplest solution," Conrad agreed. "Years of being a cop has taught me that if a person is afraid, deep down in their gut, there's no sense in running around the block searching for a concrete reason. It's better to treat the problem before it can cause a problem and figure out why it happened later. If Bertha turns out to be harmless, well then, she's had a free, if short, trip to Alaska. If she's not harmless...well, we've sent her off. No need to wait around and find out what she's planning."

Sarah glanced down at her right arm and rubbed the band-aid hiding beneath her sleeve. "Problems seem to find us no matter where we go," she said, thinking back to the hot springs. "Remember when Amanda and I were fighting that deadly virus? And now every week we have to have our blood tested." Sarah looked up. "Your husband may be right to worry about you getting into trouble, but I would rather send Bertha away before she can become another virus to worry about."

Amanda felt relief wash her worries away. "You two will honestly deal with my hubby when he returns from London?" she asked.

"We promise," Sarah said and patted Amanda's arm.

"Cross our hearts," Conrad smiled and then nodded toward the front window. "I doubt we'll be seeing Bertha anytime soon, anyway. This snowstorm is going to be with us for a while. The roads leading in and out of Snow Falls are going to be impassable."

"Well...that is true," Amanda replied, feeling hope rise in her heart. "Oh, maybe I'm acting a bit too silly," she said, trying to calm down. "Here I am fretting over my hubby becoming angry at me over a woman whose memory I've let scare me for far too long. Let him become angry if he will...because when Bertha does arrive, we'll all three send her packing."

"That's my girl," Sarah smiled. "Now, who is up for a game of Scrabble?"

"Not me," Amanda said and pointed at Conrad, "He cheats."

"I do not cheat," Conrad protested.

"Oh really?" Amanda asked, forcing Bertha away from her worried mind, "then do tell me, sir, how the word lateritious is spelled with only one 'i.' Last time I checked there were two 'i's."

Sarah sighed, sipped at her coffee, and settled back on the couch and waited for the debate of the century to begin. "It's laterous, not lateritious. The word requires one 'i,' not two," Conrad corrected Amanda.

"Rubbish! Not according to the dictionary."

"The dictionary is wrong," Conrad replied and polished off his brownie. "My word was legal."

Amanda threw both hands up in the air, nearly spilled her coffee, and exclaimed: "You cheated!"

"I did not cheat," Conrad griped. "My word was legal."

"Maybe in New York where you yanks like to swan around telling everyone to Fuhgeddaboudit." Amanda rolled her eyes. "Forget about what, for crying out loud?"

Sarah smiled and glanced at Conrad, who could be touchy about his Scrabble prowess. "Forget about your dry muffins, for starters," he muttered into his coffee mug.

"Dry...muffins?" Amanda asked. "Did you just call my perfectly baked scones...dry muffins?"

Conrad froze. "Uh...maybe I better go refill my coffee," he said, realizing he had pushed Amanda too far.

"I would run," Sarah giggled.

Conrad stood up uneasily. "I'll be right back," he said in a careful voice.

Amanda pointed her coffee cup at Conrad. "Get the Scrabble board ready, yank," she ordered him, "because this dry muffin is going to kick your can, as you Americans say."

Conrad eased toward the kitchen. "How about...Monopoly instead?" he asked and hurried away.

Amanda giggled. "Your hubby can face down a deadly criminal but is scared of little ol' me."

Sarah laughed and stood up to stretch her legs. "Good thing he's got me to keep him safe from the likes of you," she joked. Sarah walked over to the fireplace with her coffee and examined the wedding photos framed on the mantle. One photo displayed a very happy Sarah and Conrad eating a piece of wedding cake together. "We've come a long way," she smiled.

"Yes, you have, love," Amanda agreed. She stood up and walked over to Sarah. "I always knew you and Conrad would end up as one heart."

"I know, June Bug, and I'm very grateful," Sarah said in a soft voice. "Conrad makes me very happy. We love each other and accept each other for who we are...as people...cops...Christians...and husband and wife. I'm very blessed to have found love again."

"Sometimes," Amanda admitted, "I'm afraid to lose the love I have. I'm afraid of what would happen if I lost...my husband. That's why I agreed to let Bertha stay at the cabin. My husband has always taken care of me and he loves me...but lately I've put a real strain on his heart. Every adventure you and I end up on is like a weight pulling him down. I don't want to be a burden to him. If...if having Bertha watch over me makes him feel better, who am I to say no?" Amanda sighed. "I'm afraid he might grow tired of my adventures here and insist we move back to London—or worse, divorce me and leave me altogether."

"Oh June Bug, he would never do that," Sarah promised. "Your husband couldn't live a day without you. Now, sure, we've both caused our husbands some worry, but that's where love comes in, June Bug. When two people love each other they work through life's ups and downs together." Sarah gently reached out and hugged Amanda. "For better or for worse, right? Besides, our problems are over with. Honestly, what could be worse than being exposed to that awful virus?"

Amanda felt a smile touch her lips. "Nothing," she admitted. "It does seem like after that, all other problems are minor, doesn't it, love?"

"Yes," Sarah agreed, remembering sitting in a hot springs, feeling the waters burn the deadly virus out of her body. "Now, let's not worry about anything else tonight. We'll go into the kitchen, play Monopoly until four in the morning, drink coffee until we burst, and then pass out dreaming of boardwalks and top hats."

"Deal," Amanda agreed and began to walk off toward the kitchen with Sarah. As she did, the living room phone rang.

"I'll get it," Sarah said and hurried to answer the phone. "Hello...why, yes, she's here...Who is this?" Sarah's eyes went wide. She threw her hand over the phone. "It's...Bertha," she whispered. "She's at the police station."

"What?" Amanda gasped.

Sarah lowered her hand. "Uh...Amanda is...unavailable to come to the phone right now...Oh, I see...well, the roads are very bad and we—yes, I understand...But perhaps it would be best to have Andrew drive you to the local hotel for the night?"

Amanda gulped down her coffee and waited.

"I understand you've had a very long trip, ma'am, but because of the weather I'm afraid it's far too dangerous to risk the roads—no, please don't have anyone drive you to my cabin..." Sarah looked at Amanda with wide eyes and then focused back on the call. "Have the nice police man drive you to the local inn and we'll figure out something tomorrow...Yes, I'll tell Amanda to call you. Goodnight." Sarah put down the phone. "June Bug," she said, "you were right...that woman is crafty as a black widow spider."

"And now she's in our town," Amanda said and plodded toward the kitchen to refill her coffee. It was going to be a very long night.

CHAPTER TWO

Conrad called Andrew as soon as Sarah hung up the phone. Andrew was sitting in his office staring across his desk at a little old lady who made his skin crawl. "Yeah, the storm is getting worse," he told Conrad in a worried voice. "Tom just ran his last plow run for the night about an hour ago. I'll be heading home on my snowmobile if Tom doesn't make it out by morning. I hate pulling the night shift, but fair is fair." Andrew kept his eyes on Bertha. The woman was staring at him with eyes colder than the storm outside.

"How did Bertha get to the station house?" Conrad asked.

"Some crazy cabbie from Fairbanks looking to make a few extra dollars hooked a plow to his truck and drove her in," Andrew explained. "I figured he was probably some low-life if he was dumb enough to take a drive like that. He looked like he spent time in prison for running drugs. I ran his plates and—"

"He was a very nice young man," Bertha snapped at Andrew in a thick British accent that sounded rotten with malice. Bertha raised her sturdy wooden cane and shook it at Andrew. "Watch your tongue."

Andrew leaned back in his chair and studied Bertha. The old woman was wearing her gray hair wrapped in a tight bun that seemed to pull her wrinkled face into an ugly, sour lemon. Her teeth were somewhat crooked, and her breath smelled awful, like rotted fish. The woman perched on the chair in his office was wearing a thick brown coat but even through that layer he could see her frame was skeletal, like an aged bird. Somehow, Andrew was sure she wasn't wearing a comfortable, soft old granny dress underneath that coat. "Conrad, I can't take this woman to the hotel...Sarah should have asked before she offered that option...Looks like she's going to be spending the night here at the station."

"I insist you take me to—" Bertha began to declare.

Andrew held up a quick hand. "Ma'am, I would drive you to the governor's mansion for the night if I could, but the roads are impassable with the winds kicking up the snow drifts, and they will remain that way until the plows tackle everything tomorrow. Until then, I'm the cop on

DANGER IN THE SNOW

duty for the town and I'm not risking getting my truck stuck in a drift."

Bertha huffed and leaned back. She said nothing but her haughty eyes held nothing but contempt for the officer.

Listening in to Andrew's conversation over the phone, Conrad looked over at the kitchen table. Sarah and Amanda were watching him. "Just keep her at the station house, Andrew. I'll be down as soon as the plow runs out my way."

"What choice do I have?" Andrew sighed and grabbed his coffee. "I just had to switch night shifts with you, didn't I? If only I had stayed on my schedule."

"You're the one who wanted last Thursday night off to take your wife into Fairbanks. But don't sweat it, you guys needed the time together. I'm glad you drove into Fairbanks and got out of town for a while."

Andrew eyed Bertha and lowered his voice to an undertone. "Me and the wife did have a good time," he agreed, "but what a price I'm paying now."

Conrad grinned. He felt sorry for Andrew sitting in his office, stuck all night in his itchy chief's uniform catering to the whims of a cranky old woman. "I'll be down as soon as I can."

"Yeah, yeah," Andrew said and began to hang up. But then he caught himself. "Say, Conrad?"

"Yeah?"

Andrew turned around in his chair and faced his office window. "This woman seemed very determined to get to Amanda's cabin. Anything I should know about?"

"Amanda says Bertha is bad news, so be careful of her," Conrad warned. "And don't fall for any sweet little old lady tricks, either. Amanda said that Bertha can sweet-talk a grizzly out of a fish."

Andrew glanced over his shoulder and saw her cruel eyes looking at him. "Conrad, are we talking about the same woman?" he asked.

"What do you mean?"

"The woman sitting in my office looks mean enough to scare a grizzly out of his den," Andrew whispered. "She looks like a rotted prune with dead eyes."

"I heard that," Bertha snapped and knocked her cane into the side of Andrew's desk sharply. "How dare you!"

Andrew turned back around. "Lady," he said, trying to remain polite, "you want to eavesdrop on an officer of the law and then get mad about what you hear, I'd be happy to arrest you. If not, you can get yourself out of my office, you hear me? I'm not obligated to help you by law. Out of courtesy, I will let you stay the night in one of the jail cells, but come morning it sounds like you're headed out of town."

"I'll do no such thing," Bertha yelled and whacked Andrew's desk with her cane again.

Conrad heard Bertha yelling at Andrew. He gave Sarah a confused look. "Lady, if you hit my desk again, I'll lock you up for misdemeanor assault, is that clear?" Andrew told Bertha in a tone that made her sit back and shut up—for the time being. "Conrad, I'll talk to you when the roads clear."

"Yeah," Conrad said and rubbed the back of his neck, "I'll be down to the station house as soon as I can. In the meantime, keep a close eye on that woman."

"Will do."

"And also," Conrad added in a quick voice, "inform her that come morning she isn't to come within a hundred feet of Amanda."

"You're making my night just dandy, aren't you?" Andrew told Conrad with a chuckle and ended the call.

Conrad put down the telephone and walked over to the kitchen table. "Amanda, whoever is sitting in Andrew's office isn't some little old lady set on charming her way into everyone's good graces." Conrad picked up a cup of coffee and took a sip. "The woman I heard in the background snapped at Andrew and she sounded mean as a starving wolf."

Amanda felt a chill crawl down her back. "So it's

true...she has come to punish me," she whispered. "Now that she's away from London she can show her true colors."

"Suggestions?" Sarah asked Conrad in a tone that told him she was in police mode.

"I told Andrew to tell Bertha she isn't allowed within a hundred feet of Amanda," Conrad explained. "There's not much more I can do unless she breaks the law or makes a verbal threat. All we can do is hope she gets the message and leaves town."

"Conrad, how did Bertha even get into town?" Sarah asked.

Conrad sat down and glanced at Mittens. Mittens was chewing on a rawhide bone and tussling on the warm rug near the fire. "Andrew said some ex-con wanting money hooked a plow to his truck and drove her in."

"All the way from Fairbanks?" Sarah asked.

"Some cabbie with a record for running drugs," Conrad said with a shrug. "Some guy named Robbie Nelson."

"That makes me wonder how Bertha found a person like that to begin with," Sarah pointed out. "Was he just hanging out at the airport waiting to get picked up by the cops for endangering the lives of sweet old ladies? Besides, an old lady wouldn't take a ride from a guy who looked like an ex-con." Sarah looked at Amanda. "Maybe not so sweet. Looks like you were right, June Bug. Not that I doubted you."

"You had every right to doubt me," Amanda replied. "I did act a bit...dramatic. But at least now you can understand why."

"Put your mind at ease," Conrad assured Amanda. "Bertha will not come near you."

"Oh, she'll find a way," Amanda warned Conrad.

"What do you mean, June Bug?" Sarah asked.

Amanda took a sip of coffee. "Bertha will call my husband," she said. "My husband, as loving as he is, will insist I take her in. She'll play the stranded little old lady card—oh poor me, I just need a place to stay for a few nights, sorry to trouble you, kind sir. If I resist...oh, he'll think the worst of me. I can deal with that, I suppose. But with his father being so sick...and with me falling into trouble nearly every step...oh, my husband will give me an ear full." Amanda sighed. "My father-in-law is honestly sick...if I cause him trouble with Bertha...? No, it's better if I handle Bertha on my own...somehow."

"Honey," Sarah said, "marriages are built to manage problems, not ignore them. You can't hide this problem with Bertha from him just because he's dealing with a sick parent."

"You don't understand, Los Angeles," Amanda explained

in a desperate voice, "it's not just that his dad is sick. My father-in-law, he...well, he despises the ground I walk on."

"Why?" Conrad asked. "You're a decent woman."

"Not in the eyes of a man who wanted his son to marry a posh London socialite," Amanda told Conrad. "His parents assumed he would marry a lovely girl from another rich English family...my hubby married a middle-class girl instead." Amanda took a glum sip of her coffee. "My hubby and I have done well for ourselves. It's not like we're alley beggars."

"You're a very talented and special woman," Sarah assured Amanda.

"I'm very loved," Amanda replied in a grateful voice. "But money-wise...my father-in-law never thought I was good enough for his son, not even after you gave me half of your fortune."

"Not a fortune, honey," Sarah smiled, "just royalties from my books that you deserved to have."

"That's a fortune to me," Amanda said in a grateful voice. "Money was starting to get a little tight," she continued. "It's expensive to fly back and forth to London from Anchorage. But now, because of you, I can be relaxed. I can even have a grand shopping trip in London. Our cabin is paid off and money is put up for my son. But," Amanda finished, "it wouldn't matter if I had a billion dollars...it wouldn't be good enough for my hubby's daddy because I simply don't have the right society pedigree. And if my husband was called home to mediate a fight between me and Bertha, well, his father would probably start a war."

"But earlier you agreed—" Conrad began to speak.

"I know I agreed to send Bertha packing," Amanda told Conrad. "That was when she was still in Fairbanks. Now she's too close for comfort, and I'm sure she's going to call my husband and make it worse."

Before anyone could speak a word the telephone next to the refrigerator rang. "I'll answer it," Conrad said and hurried over to the phone. "Hello? Oh...yeah...right here." Conrad held the phone out. "Guess who?"

"My hubby?" Amanda moaned. Conrad nodded. Amanda eased up to her feet, crept over to the phone, and took it from Conrad. "Hello love, how is your father?...Resting? That's good...What? Bertha? Oh, I heard she's holed up at the police station for the night...real bad snowstorm here...what's that? Bertha was told she can't come near me? Well...dear...my love...I told you how I felt about Bertha...I'm not acting childish...I know your father is sick...I know I almost died..." Amanda felt her heart sink. "Love, please listen to reason...I didn't ask you to send Bertha...I'm not a child..."

Sarah saw Amanda go from upset to angry. "Stand back,"

she warned Conrad. Conrad stepped away from the refrigerator.

"Now you listen to me...I didn't ask you to send that awful woman to babysit me...Sarah is my friend! It wasn't her fault...no, you're not listening. Love...it wasn't my fault some deranged woman set a virus loose in the hot springs I wanted to buy...no, you listen! I was sitting here worried about upsetting you, but if you're going to act like a...a jerk...then you can go soak your head in the snow. And one more thing. Bertha can take a hike!" Amanda slammed down the phone, looked at Sarah, and then burst out crying. "Now I've done it!"

Sarah ran over to Amanda. "Girl time," she whispered to Conrad. Conrad nodded and left the kitchen. "Now, now," Sarah told Amanda and walked her friend back to the kitchen table. "Your hubby will understand...you were just upset and hung up on him in the heat of the moment. I'm sure you'll make up when he calls back."

"He refused to listen to reason...he's blaming you...he's blaming me...he's treating me like a child," Amanda cried.

"He's only worried, honey," Sarah told Amanda. "Conrad and I had an argument the day I left for the hot springs with you. And now look at us...right as rain. Stormy seas soon settle, I promise."

Amanda lifted her teary eyes up to Sarah. "My father-in-law is going to turn my hubby against me. I can see his hand in this mess already."

"June Bug, I know your husband. He's a good man who loves you very much. I'm sure he'll see reason."

Amanda wiped at her tears. She began to speak but then the phone rang again. Sarah quickly answered the call, expecting it to be Amanda's husband. Instead it was Andrew. "Hello? Oh...hi, Andrew."

"Sorry to bother you, Sarah," Andrew said in a heavy voice, "but I wanted to let you know. I tried my hardest, but I couldn't keep her."

"Keep who...you mean Bertha?" Sarah asked.

"Sarah, that woman insisted I allow her to leave the station. I...kinda lost my temper and let her. I had Michael drive her to the hotel." Andrew scratched the back of his neck and then loosened the button at his collar. "That old lady...I never saw anything so mean and ugly in all my life, Sarah. I could have thrown her out in the snow with my bare hands. I was more than happy to let her leave. Besides, I had no legal way to hold her at the station. We don't have a restraining order against her or anything."

"How long ago was this?" Sarah asked.

"Not more than two minutes. Michael is driving off with

her right now," Andrew explained and then added: "I have some more bad news."

"I'm all ears."

"That old lady told me she has no intention of leaving Snow Falls. As a matter of fact, she told me she's thinking about moving here," Andrew told Sarah. "How? Who knows. But the one thing I'm sure of is that she's out to get Amanda. When I told her she couldn't go near Amanda she dared me to stop her."

"Really?"

Andrew nodded. "I wish I could have arrested her right then and there, but on what grounds? She didn't exactly threaten her. Being an ornery old fishwife isn't a crime. I have to wait until she breaks the law first. You and I both know that's the hardest part about being a cop."

"Yeah, I know," Sarah nodded. "We have to let some known criminals run free until they break the law. Even then they have every rat attorney begging to defend them."

"Keep a close eye on Amanda," Andrew told Sarah. "I'm going to call her husband in London and tell him what's going on and ask why in the world he sent that woman here."

"Uh...well, good idea," Sarah agreed. "Maybe it'll do that

man good to hear the truth from an outside party. Make sure you tell him every word Bertha said to you."

"Will do," Andrew promised. "I'll be in touch."

"Thanks for calling, Andrew," Sarah said in a grateful voice. "You're a real friend."

"Don't thank me yet," Andrew replied, "we still have trouble in town. I'll be in touch."

Sarah put down the phone and returned to the table. "Bertha insisted Andrew let her go. Andrew had no choice. He's having Michael drive her to the hotel on his snowmobile."

"Good grief."

"But don't worry," Sarah said, "Andrew is going to call your hubby and tell him just what kind of woman Bertha is."

"He is?"

"Now the blame falls on that awful woman and away from you. And that," Sarah said and hugged Amanda's worried shoulders, "should make your hubby see reason. Now, let's have some more coffee and settle down for the night."

Amanda wiped tears from her eyes. "I told you Bertha

was an awful woman," she said into the telephone. "No...it's okay, love...I know you meant well. Bertha can be a real snake charmer. No, haven't heard a word from her...if I do, I'll send her packing right back to London...don't be sorry...I love you, too." Amanda looked at Sarah with relief in her eyes. Her hubby had called to express concern and remorse after speaking with Andrew and getting a better picture of the situation.

Sarah saw the relief quickly turn to anger. Amanda's husband confessed a dark secret. "Your daddy did what?...He was the one who insisted you send Bertha to Alaska?...What do you mean, Bertha spoke with him? Oh, I'm going to kick that awful man in his leg!"

Sarah leaned against the kitchen counter, took a careful sip of coffee, and listened to every word Amanda spoke. Something smelled fishy and she didn't like it. "What do you mean, Bertha visited your daddy before we arrived...how many times...? Well, why didn't you say something? No, I'm not mad at you...oh, this is all so frustrating. I don't like being kept in the dark." Amanda looked at Sarah with confused eyes. "Your father truly hates me...oh yes, he does and you know it...can you finally admit that? Good...What?...Oh, okay. Call me back...but not until morning. I need time to sleep and calm down...yes, I love you...night, love." Amanda put down the phone and threw her hands onto her hips. "Seems like a conspiracy was formed against me before my husband and I even returned to London."

"You've been on the phone with your husband for half an hour," Sarah pointed out gently, wanting to know more. "I didn't catch the entire conversation."

Amanda dropped her hands from her hips, strolled over to the kitchen table, and plopped down. "Well, Andrew called my husband, as planned," she explained and grabbed a brownie off of her white plate, "and Andrew told my hubby exactly what he thought of Bertha."

Sarah watched Amanda take a bite of brownie as the winds cried and howled. "I'm all ears, June Bug."

"You know Andrew and my hubby are good friends, right?"

"Andrew is a good man," Sarah nodded. "The entire town respects him as a friend."

"Yeah, he's a good bloke," Amanda agreed. "My hubby doesn't get along with just anyone. He's a picky fish." Amanda took another bite of her brownie. "So Andrew told him how awful Bertha was, which didn't add more blue to an already gray sky. But my hubby respects Andrew and listened to him. Andrew drove the truth into his stubborn mind, which finally made him open up about some hidden secrets."

Sarah walked to the back door, checked the snow drifts accumulating against the cars in the driveway, and then made her way over to Amanda. "Storm is getting worse," she pointed out. "I'm surprised we still have power. The only good thing is that there's nothing moving out there. I doubt we'll be seeing Bertha anytime soon."

Amanda watched Sarah sit down. "It's clear that Bertha manipulated my father-in-law and then manipulated my husband into the bargain. It was no coincidence that she was at the agency when we arrived. It's also clear that Bertha has traveled to America to complete her threat."

"It does seem that way, doesn't it?" Sarah asked. She sat down and looked at Mittens. Mittens was sound asleep. "What are these secrets he revealed to you, June Bug?"

"Well," Amanda said in a disbelieving tone of voice, "my wonderful hubby told me that Bertha began visiting his daddy about six months ago. She was assigned to him as a home visit nurse for some follow-up care. Now," Amanda pointed out, "that part could have been merely coincidental. Who knows? But let me tell you, once she found out I was in the picture...oh, what must have gone through her sick and diseased mind? And let's not forget that my father-in-law despises me, so he didn't exactly have an incentive to leash a rabid dog when he saw one."

"I'm sorry, honey."

Amanda polished off her brownie. "My hubby told me that Bertha retired from being his daddy's home nurse about a week before we arrived in London. Why? Who knows, probably another coincidence, right? Well...at least that's what I first thought. You cops are rubbing off on me." Amanda studied the brownie plate and went for her coffee instead. "By resigning her position, Bertha must have known my husband would hire another home nurse for his father, which means a nice and convenient trip to the agency to interview for a replacement...where she would be waiting."

"You're turning into a regular detective," Sarah replied, impressed. "Keep painting the scene, Matlock."

Amanda blushed a little and then continued. "Years and years of repressed anger inside of her," she said, "and then all of a sudden Bertha finds a doorway that opens up into an opportunity perfect for what she wants...for what she needs...revenge. So, what does she do? She carefully plots out the perfect scheme, begins manipulating my weak father-in-law with her diseased charm, making sure he will help her control any opposition...and then...she strikes!" Amanda hit the table with her fist. "Like a black widow going after its mate."

Sarah would have laughed at her best friend's dramatic narrative, but instead she simply nodded. Amanda had laid out a perfect scene and it felt right in line with her gut. "That sounds right, June Bug."

Amanda leaned back in her chair and folded her arms. "The worst part is...until that awful woman commits a crime, there is nothing we can do. My hubby has informed Andrew to tell her that she is not to come anywhere near me or our cabin. But who knows the mental state this woman is in? Why, she might try and kill me regardless. She's clearly not swayed by threats of legal consequences."

Sarah studied Amanda's eyes and saw a very deep worry. "Honey, does this woman have any children?"

"Not that I'm aware of," Amanda said. "She surely didn't while she was turning my innocent years into a living nightmare. She would have been in her late fifties or so at that time...she never mentioned a son or daughter or grandchild, never mentioned any family at all. She never left to visit anyone, either."

Sarah took a sip of coffee, considering everything. "Okay," she said, "let's review what we know."

"Okay."

"Bertha is a registered nurse, right?" Sarah asked.

"Unfortunately."

"And she's between sixty-five and seventy years old?" Sarah asked.

"I guess, love," Amanda replied. "I never knew her exact age."

"Andrew said Bertha appeared to be around seventy, so let's run with that," Sarah said and continued. "We know Bertha became a home nurse to your father-in-law, either by chance or by deliberation." Amanda nodded. "We know Bertha came to the realization that you were her patient's daughter-in-law."

"Boy did she ever."

Sarah worked on her coffee. "So what does this awful woman do, at the moment of that realization?" she asked.

"I'll tell you what she did," Amanda said in a worried voice, "she walked back through time and remembered a dark threat she made against an innocent young woman and decided to fulfill her promise. She carried an evil grudge all these years and saw her opportunity to get back at me, once and for all."

"I wish I could find a flaw in your reasoning, June Bug, but I can't. It does appear that Bertha is in town to cause harm," Sarah told Amanda. She put down her coffee and looked at the kitchen window. "Until that woman leaves Snow Falls, you're not leaving my sight. Also, I want you to begin carrying a gun."

"I...have a gun in my suitcase," Amanda confessed. "I loathe those awful things and can't wait until the day all weapons are hammered into plowshares like the Bible says."

"Unfortunately, for the time being, the bad guys are still out there, and the good guys still need a way to defend themselves," Sarah pointed out. "Gang members, criminals, thugs, drug dealers...they'll find a way to get guns regardless of what laws are passed, and meanwhile law-abiding citizens like us are left to suffer the consequences. For now, we carry our guns not because we want to but because we have to defend our lives in a very dangerous world."

"From bows and arrows and spears to guns and bombs...mankind has sure improved, huh, love? We create more ways to kill than to heal and more ways to hate than to love." Amanda sighed. "Long ago, I once believed Bertha had a decent heart inside her, and I thought if I simply bent to her will I would find a loving nanny under her hard exterior, ready to cherish and protect me. But then she removed her mask and I saw the monster lurking underneath. There was nothing I could do to make her happy. She didn't want me to obey her, she wanted me to suffer. And now that monster is in town and there's no telling what weapons she has hidden in her valise."

Sarah nodded. "I remember once, when I was a rookie...real wet behind the ears...I believed only cops and government officials should carry guns. I believed we were responsible for protecting the civilian population and that civilians didn't need guns."

"What happened to change your mind?"

Sarah picked up her coffee. "A man tried to snatch a three-year-old girl from her mother in the parking lot of a grocery store. No cop was around." Sarah closed her eyes and saw a vicious monster trying to steal a precious child from her mother. "The man had a knife...but the mother had a gun in her purse. Her husband was a cop who insisted she carry a gun and taught her how to use it. Long story short, this woman shot the man trying to steal her daughter."

"Good for her!" Amanda cheered.

"The man ended up six feet under," Sarah smiled. "And, as it turns out, he was a convicted felon who had recently been paroled from prison who had no intention of obeying the law. Now, what would have happened if the woman hadn't had a gun?"

"I shudder to imagine."

"Me too," Sarah said. "And it was on that very day that I realized the wisdom of our country's laws, and why every person has the right to carry a firearm and defend themselves. When a country is at war, you don't throw rocks at enemy tanks, and when a person's life is in danger, you have a right to fight back on equal footing."

"I agree completely," Amanda said. "I guess...I'll start carrying my gun in my purse."

"I prefer an ankle holster, but a purse is fine, too." Sarah finished off her coffee. "You can't be shy with a gun, June Bug. Don't be afraid to go with your gut – sometimes that means we shoot first and ask questions later. Especially when there seems to be a clear and present threat in town."

"Oh," Amanda fretted, "I don't want to kill Bertha...I only want her to...well...shoo."

"Doesn't seem that Bertha has any intent of leaving town anytime soon," Sarah pointed out.

Amanda sighed. "I know."

Sara stood up and refilled her coffee. "June Bug, we need to find out if this woman has any connections – maybe some family she didn't mention. She's in her seventies, and from what Andrew said, she's not exactly spry and robust. That leads me to believe she may not be working alone."

Amanda's eyes grew wide. "Do you honestly think?" she asked. "I mean, I never considered the idea that Bertha might be teaming up with a deranged husband or evil offspring. Goodness..."

Sarah looked toward the kitchen entrance. "Conrad is in the bedroom working on one of his puzzles. I need to go update him and have him run Bertha's name to see if she has any known associates."

Amanda gave Sarah a loving look. "Los Angeles, thank you," she said in a sincere voice.

"For what?"

"For believing me. For caring and being a real friend...no, a sister," Amanda explained and nearly began crying. "When my hubby took me away from London and moved us to Alaska, I never imagined I would find a real sister...a real family. But you and Conrad honestly care about me and for that...thank you." Amanda wiped at a tear. "I never feel alone when I'm with you. I always feel safe and loved, and that's a gift that you can't put a price tag on."

Sarah walked over to Amanda and hugged her. "You're the one who helped give our coffee shop life. You changed the coffee shop from a rugged wreck into a cozy, inviting place."

Amanda laughed. "Well, that coffee shop was a little on the drab side," she said and looked up at Sarah. "And speaking of the coffee shop, we better begin opening the doors for the winter."

"I opened up the coffee shop all last week while you were gone," Sarah smiled. "The regulars poured in, complained about my coffee, talked about this and that, ate me out of cinnamon rolls, and then wandered away."

"The folks in this town complain about your coffee but still keep coming back."

"Guess my coffee isn't that bad," Sarah laughed and hugged Amanda again. "June Bug, I love you very deeply. Having you in my life is a blessing. Conrad feels the same way. Why, if he didn't have someone to fuss at while playing Scrabble his life might come to an end."

"Conrad cheats at Scrabble," Amanda whispered and hugged Sarah back.

"He does seem to get his I's and E's confused, doesn't he?" Sarah grinned.

"He sure does," Amanda nodded. "And—" Amanda quit speaking when the telephone rang. "I told that husband of mine to give me time to calm down."

"I'll answer the call," Sarah said and hurried over to the phone. "Hello?...Oh, hi Andrew."

"Sarah, I've got some bad news," Andrew said in an upset tone of voice, heaving a deep sigh.

"What's the matter?" Sarah asked.

"That old lady we wanted out of town...well, she's dead."

"Dead?" Sarah asked.

Amanda jumped to her feet and ran to Sarah. "Who's dead?" she asked.

"Bertha," Sarah said in a daze. "Andrew, what happened?"

"I'll explain later. Right now, I need Conrad down at the station. And you better come, too, Sarah. I hate to ask this of you both when the storm is so bad, but I'll feel a lot better if we have two detectives on this murder case instead of one. She's a British citizen so we'll have the feds asking questions as soon as we file our report, so we have to get the investigation done right."

"Andrew, the storm outside is getting worse," Sarah pointed out. "I don't even think we could dig out my truck if we wanted to. It's coming down too fast."

"Better dig out your snowmobiles," Andrew replied in a heavy voice, "because I've got one wounded cop and a dead woman on my hands."

"Wounded cop?"

"Someone struck Michael in the back of the head before they shot the old woman in the back two times," Andrew explained.

"At the hotel?"

"Yeah, at the hotel," Andrew confirmed. "Right out front. Because of the storm, no one saw or heard anything."

Sarah took Amanda's hand. "I'll have Conrad call you right back, Andrew."

"Have him call me here at the station," Andrew instructed. "I called Brent in. When he gets here to man the station house I'll head over to the hotel. Brent should be here in about twenty minutes."

"Will do," Sarah said and hung up the phone. She looked at Amanda. "Bertha has been shot. She is dead."

Amanda grew very silent and still. When she finally

spoke, her voice came out very, very scared. "Whoever killed Bertha will try and kill me next," she whispered.

Sarah looked at the kitchen window and watched the storm swirl as the winds howled across the landscape. "Another snowstorm...another murder...and just when we thought all of our troubles were over with."

Outside in the dark, stormy night, a figure was racing away from the hotel on a snowmobile, headed straight for Amanda's cabin. "One down, one to go. It's time to pay the price," the voice growled as the storm raged on.

CHAPTER THREE

Conrad was not pleased at the prospect of digging out a frozen snowmobile from a snow-covered shed then heading to town through a storm. But a murder had been committed, and his job required him to be on the scene. "I'll call you from the hotel," he promised Sarah, slapping on his leather jacket.

Sarah grabbed a thick black ski coat and placed it over his leather jacket and then helped Conrad put on a black balaclava ski mask and a pair of thick winter gloves. Conrad would have preferred his old hunting jacket to the modern insulated winter gear that Sarah made him wear, but he had to admit that being warm was better than retaining his image and freezing into the bargain.

Then Sarah took down her own snow parka and began to dress for the snowstorm. "I can ride with you. Andrew asked me to come down."

"We only have the one snowmobile," Conrad pointed out, now starting to sweat under his balaclava. Mittens raised her head at the commotion in the kitchen and tilted her head at the strangely dressed man standing by the door, then laid back down and went to sleep. "Besides, what about Amanda? We can't fit three on a snowmobile, and we can't leave her here alone. If the power goes off, you need to be here to start the generator. We don't need our pipes freezing up on us." He did not voice his concern that Sarah might need to protect Amanda from other, more sinister dangers, but Sarah understood the worry in his eyes.

Sarah loved Conrad for trying to protect her and her friend. She gently kissed his cheek, getting a mouthful of woolly lint, and opened the back door. An icy wind followed by screaming snow raced into the kitchen like a prowler searching for innocent victims. "Be careful," she begged.

"Will do," Conrad yelled over the winds and hurried outside into the dark storm.

"Please do," Sarah whispered and pushed the back door closed with her back. "Well, June Bug, it looks like it's just the two of us."

Amanda glanced down at a sturdy box on the table that she had retrieved from her cabin on her way home from the airport. She looked up at Sarah. "My gun is in this box," she said in a voice full of dread. "My gun is in this box...my hubby and my son are in London...your husband just went out into the storm to help catch a killer...what a night."

Sarah walked over to the kitchen window and looked out. She looked toward the shed, waited, and then saw a dim light turn on. "Conrad is in the shed," she said and waited. A few minutes later she saw a pair of headlights flash out into the blowing snow from the open door of the shed. "He got the snowmobile out." Sarah watched as Conrad drove a white and blue snowmobile out into the storm. A little ways down the driveway, he hopped off, ran back into the shed, shut off the light and closed the door. He peered toward the cabin then and waved at her before he raced off to the snowmobile and was off into the storm. "And now he's gone."

"Come sit down, love."

Sarah sighed. "I think I'll have more coffee," she replied and walked over to the kitchen counter. "All we can do now is wait."

"Waiting is horrible...not knowing is even more horrible," Amanda commented. "I suppose there's no sense in making it worse, though."

Sarah refilled her coffee cup and leaned back against the kitchen counter. She stood still for a minute and listened to the storm howl and whine. "Isn't it funny, June Bug? When I was living in Los Angeles, I would have been excited to see just a few snowflakes in the air...not that it ever happened. Now if I see a few snowflakes in the air I prepare myself for a hard winter. But the strange thing is...now I look forward to the hard winters. At first when I moved to Snow Falls, I missed Southern California...the warm sun, city living, the beaches, the palm trees and the hills and canyons...a part of me still does, I guess. But when winter arrives here, I feel a sense of dread and excitement, both at the same time."

"I love the snow," Amanda confessed. "Not all the time. The winters in Snow Falls can be very long and scary, you're right about that, love. Yet when spring begins to arrive, I start to feel sad. I hate saying goodbye to the snow. As much as I fuss about the cold...well, the snow is my friend. It always breaks my heart to see it melt away." Amanda kept her eyes on the sturdy cardboard box in front of her. "The rain and fog that always shuffled around London with me were old friends, too. The rain and fog somehow seemed to transform the world into my own special place...a hidden world that only I understood. Silly, huh?"

"Not at all," Sarah replied. "That's how the snow makes me feel. The sun and palm trees in Southern California seemed to belong to everyone...but the snow, June Bug, is ours." Sarah sipped at her coffee and listened to the storm. "I wish my friend Pete were here. I wish he hadn't changed his mind about leaving California. But Pete belongs in Los Angeles with his cigars and Chinese take-

DANGER IN THE SNOW

out. And I belong in Alaska with the snow and the bears." Sarah stared into the swirling snow outside the windows and saw the form of a creepy snowman in a leather jacket appear in her mind, grinning with familiar malice. *"Hello Sarah,"* the apparition hissed as it pulled a peppermint candy cane out of one of its pockets. *"Almost got you with the virus, didn't I? I come in all forms, oh yes I do."*

"Love?" Amanda asked, spotting a strange expression cross Sarah's face.

"Huh?" Sarah asked.

"Are you okay? You look like you just saw a ghost."

"I guess I did," Sarah whispered. She walked over to the kitchen table and sat down. "Maybe we better look at your gun, June Bug. I would like to make sure it's loaded properly and ready to fire."

"Oh...okay," Amanda said reluctantly, like someone was pulling a band-aid slowly and painfully off of an injury she didn't want to touch. She reached out her hands and removed the lid of the box. She set the top down and reached into the box to pick up the microfiber cloth she used to wrap the gun when it was in storage. "What the bloody...?" she said, her brow wrinkling in confusion.

"What is it?" Sarah asked.

Amanda's eyes grew wide with fear. "This," she said and

unwrapped the cloth. Inside was a roughly-shaped gray rock instead of a gun. "Love, what's going on here?"

Sarah stared at the rock and then jumped to her feet. She ran to the phone and dialed Andrew as fast as she could. Andrew picked up on the third ring. "Andrew, it's Sarah. Someone stole Amanda's gun from the safety lockbox inside her cabin."

"Are you sure?" Andrew asked, slapping on a pair of thick gray gloves.

"I'm sure," Sarah said. "Whoever stole her gun put a rock in the box to counter the weight so she wouldn't know. My guess is the person who shot Bertha stole Amanda's gun."

"Who would do that? Why would they try to frame Amanda for murder?" Andrew asked.

"I don't know, but that's what it looks like to me," Sarah told Andrew. "Listen, Conrad just left a few minute ago. He should get to the hotel soon. When he arrives, have him come back here. He needs to get to Amanda's cabin and search it for evidence."

Andrew hesitated. "Sarah, I really need him at the hotel."

"I know," Sarah said, "but Conrad needs to search Amanda's cabin, it's urgent."

"Sarah, it's hard enough moving in this storm. We have to get a dead body over to the hospital and arrange for an autopsy and the works." Andrew looked down at his messy desk. "But if you think Conrad needs to be elsewhere, I trust you, Sarah. Lord knows, your reputation as a homicide detective is one for the books."

"You're a good cop yourself, Andrew," Sarah pointed out.

"When it comes to murder, sometimes I feel I'm in way over my head," Andrew confessed. "When you and Amanda were trapped up at the hot springs, I had a killer disguised as one of my own guys and didn't even know it. I'm better at tracking down a hungry bear than a killer. Remember when I almost shot and killed Conrad?"

"You saw two men fighting in a dark, snowy alley and made a quick call," Sarah said, trying to reassure him. "Cops don't always make the right call."

"Yeah, I know," Andrew sighed heavily. "I'll send Conrad over to Amanda's cabin and see what he digs up. But if what you're saying is right, Sarah, that means the killer is still around. This doesn't look like a hit-and-run situation. Michael said he found the old woman's pocketbook and luggage lying untouched in the snow."

"At least now we have a direction to focus on," Sarah told Andrew.

"Yeah, that's true, Sarah," Andrew agreed. "The question is, how are we going to find a killer in this storm? We're back at the night I nearly shot and killed Conrad...we're all walking blind in the snow."

Sarah glanced over her shoulder toward Amanda. Amanda was studying the rock. "I know, Andrew. It seems like the killers who pay us a visit always wait until a snowstorm traps us."

"No, if that was true, then all of Alaska would be in trouble. It's just what it's like up here...too bad the snow can't keep the outside world locked out," Andrew said. He picked up a cup of coffee and took a drink. "Snow Falls is a safe, small town, Sarah. It's only been the last couple years it seems like we're headed for the record books as murder capital of the rural United States. Folks in Snow Falls don't like that kind of attention...did you know some folks have even moved away?" Andrew stared at his coffee cup. "The old-timers are staying put but the younger generation...well, they'll move away. I guess the day will come when this old town will shut down and be no more."

"Don't say that," Sarah told Andrew in a firm voice. "This is our town, and we're not going to let it die."

"Sure," Andrew sighed, "we have O'Mally's, a diner, a small hospital, a few shops, and a whole bunch of snow. Folks are just lining up to move to Snow Falls, Sarah." Andrew shook his head. "What we've been having our share of is murder and crime and that's not good for this town."

Sarah felt guilt grip her heart. "Conrad and I brought trouble...I'm sorry."

"Don't be sorry, Sarah," Andrew said in a heavy voice, "it was inevitable that trouble would find its way into Snow Falls sooner or later. Can't hide from the world forever. I better get on to the hotel."

"Have Conrad call me from Amanda's cabin, okay?"

"Will do." Andrew began to hang up but then added in a quick voice: "Oh, Sarah?"

"Yes?"

"I contacted the state police," Andrew explained.

"Let me guess, they can't move in this storm?"

"Not an inch," Andrew confirmed. "They have their hands full trying to keep the interstate open for emergency vehicles. This storm is hitting our area pretty hard. Plows were also out trying to keep old Route 144 open, but the snow was coming down too fast, so the plows were called in until it lets up."

"Wonder if the convict who drove Bertha into Snow Falls made it back to Fairbanks?" Sarah asked. "I'm wondering if that convict even left town?" Sarah rubbed her chin with her left hand.

"I've been wondering that same thing myself," Andrew said. "I'm still waiting for the London Police to send me information on Bertha. Maybe we'll find out something interesting that will help us?"

"I hope so," Sarah agreed. "Just keep up the good work."

"I'll try."

"And Andrew?" Sarah said.

"Yeah?"

"Nice work running the convict who drove Bertha into town. Your quick thinking really paid off, so don't knock yourself down into the snow, okay?" Sarah said.

"Guy just struck me as strange was all."

"You followed your gut and hit a solid target," Sarah pointed out.

"Guess I did," Andrew said, feeling a smile touch his tired lips. "Okay, Sarah, I better get out into the storm before this warm office chains me down. I'll be in touch."

"Be careful out there." Sarah hung up the phone and returned to Amanda. "What are you thinking, June Bug?"

"I'm wondering who stole my gun," Amanda confessed, examining the rock in her hands. "This rock came from the stone path leading up to my house from the driveway. I recognize this granite color. Someone must have entered my cabin while I was in London...and that tells me there was a plan in place to destroy my life long before I got back to Alaska."

Sarah studied the rock. "Andrew is waiting to hear back from the authorities over in London."

"I'm not surprised," Amanda sighed. "With the time difference, it must be the middle of the night there right now. And you know, London has changed quite a bit since I last lived there. Like the rest of the world, my old home has a lot more crime than it used to. They're probably chasing down six different major crimes and one request from a local cop in Alaska is at the bottom of their list of priorities."

"Half the time I think the increase in crime has more to do with an increase in political correctness and overly protective laws than anything else," Sarah commented, shaking her head wearily.

"I agree. Whatever happened to common sense?"

"I wonder the same thing, June Bug," Sarah replied. "I was reading an article last week about a town that shut down a little girl's lemonade stand because she didn't have a business permit and was in violation of some silly city code."

"Are you serious?" Amanda asked in a disgusted voice.

Sarah shook her head. "I'm very serious," she said and sat down. "And another thing…a few weeks ago a fire chief was fired from his job because he refused to compromise his religious beliefs." Sarah shook her head again. "It's become tough out there…been tough for a long time."

"Tell me about it," Amanda said. "And the airports. Goodness, love, the security agencies in charge of the airports treat you like you're a convict. Why, I saw one security guy actually patting down an old woman in a wheelchair. Poor lady had to be close to a hundred years old. But that wasn't the worst of it. My hubby and I actually saw a security person...a thug, really...take a baby bottle away from a mother nursing her newborn and refuse to give it back while he tested it for explosive residue! Can you even imagine? The whole time, the baby was wailing, and the man's face was stone cold. It was monstrous."

"I think they're just trying to do their jobs, but I've heard too many horror stories about airport security personnel," Sarah agreed. "Profiling, inappropriate judgment calls... but threats are waiting for us all over the world, June Bug. We're lucky there's still good people out there willing to fight the good fight. There's people like Andrew and Pete and Conrad...and you." Sarah looked around her kitchen. "It's becoming obvious that little towns like Snow Falls are the last stronghold. We'll keep fighting."

"With a hotdog in one hand at the baseball game and an apple pie cooling on the window sill," Amanda added with a grin.

"The good old days," Sarah sighed. "When my grandfather was twelve years old, he was out working the

DANGER IN THE SNOW

fields with his daddy. Kids today...oh, what's the point? Let's focus on the case."

"Kids today indeed...why work a good summer job when you could curl up with your cell phone instead?" Amanda said and turned the rock over in her hands. "But it surely wasn't a kid that killed Bertha."

"No, honey, it wasn't a kid that killed Bertha," Sarah agreed. "We're dealing with someone who understands the art of murder."

"Why do you say that?"

"Because whoever killed Bertha was waiting for her at the hotel," Sarah explained. "That person knocked Michael out cold, shot Bertha dead, and left her pocketbook untouched. We're not dealing with a street thug, June Bug. This is someone with a strategy."

Amanda looked up at Sarah. "I was afraid of that," she said in a scared voice.

Sarah reached out and patted Amanda's hand. "Honey, we're going to find the killer, I promise."

"I'm not sure I want to," Amanda confessed. "Maybe if we leave the killer alone, he'll...just leave town. Just leave us alone."

"Do you really believe that?" Sarah asked and tapped the rock sitting on the table with her index finger.

Amanda lowered her eyes. "I wish I did," she whispered, "but deep down in my heart...I know the killer has just begun his awful game."

Conrad found the front door to Amanda's cabin standing open. "Not good," he whispered, holding his gun at the ready as icy winds and heavy snow buffeted his body. "At least the power is still on."

"For now," Andrew said, studying a snow-covered front porch lit by a single fixture aimed out from the house. The cold light from the bulb cast an eerie glow out into the night, bathing the snow with a creepy presence that didn't sit well with Conrad or Andrew. "What do you think?"

Conrad glanced around. The cabin was surrounded by deep woods, sitting alone down a lonely road by itself. Sarah's place was miles away, and the nearest neighbor was at least a quarter of a mile closer to town. Amanda's husband, after living in a crowded London flat all his life, prided himself on a home that boasted absolute privacy. Privacy was nice, but it also allowed for criminals to come and go with ease. "You take the back door. I'll go in through the front."

Andrew looked at Conrad. Conrad looked like a criminal himself, wearing the black ski mask. At least the guy was finally dressing sensibly. "What do you think is going on?" he asked over the icy winds.

Conrad turned his attention to Andrew. Andrew, who had lived in Alaska his whole life, never needed to be convinced to dress sensibly for the weather. He was dressed in a thick gray and brown ski suit equipped with winter cap and a brown ski mask. Conrad had learned the hard way that riding in the snow without a ski mask was miserable, though Andrew would never make fun of him. Andrew had taught him how to manage the brutal winters and stay alive. Still, Conrad thought, he didn't like standing out in the snow with his face hidden like a criminal preparing to commit a crime. The New Yorker in him was fussy about appearances. But what could he do? It was either freeze or stay warm. "Someone is out to hurt Amanda," he said in a careful voice. "At first I thought Amanda was being a drama queen over this mess with her former nanny, but now I owe her an apology."

Andrew glanced around the dark night with his gun gripped firmly in both hands. "Amanda is a nice lady, Conrad. She's a good addition to Snow Falls, and so is her husband. Both are good people." Conrad nodded. "Can't imagine who would want to hurt them."

"Them?" Conrad asked.

"Why not?" Andrew asked back. "Maybe whoever killed that old lady and is out to hurt the wife will use the husband to accomplish the job? Or vice versa? Use the wife to go after the husband?"

Conrad hadn't considered that option. "That's possible," he told Andrew as the snow continued to attack his face. Even though he was dressed for warmth, his body was slowly turning to ice. "Let's talk more after we check out the cabin."

"Got it," Andrew said and, without saying another word, he sprinted off into the snow and vanished around the left side of the cabin into the shadows. Conrad looked around and then carefully eased up onto the front porch and began checking for boot prints. When his eyes came up empty, he focused on the front door, maneuvered over to the opening, drew in a deep breath, and then stormed into a cozy living room that looked like a seaside English cottage. Without wasting a second, he kicked the front door closed, scanned the living room, and then raced through a dark doorway, entering a lonely dining room. He saw no one and saw no hints of any entry. He moved on into a dimly lit kitchen and snatched the back door open. Andrew was waiting. He came in and they both peeled their ski masks up so they could talk and breathe easier inside the cabin.

"Look at this," Conrad said in a quick voice once they turned the lights on in the kitchen.

Andrew hurried over and looked down at the polished

DANGER IN THE SNOW

hardwood floor. He saw small puddles of wet snow. "Someone's been in here."

"Back door was unlocked," Conrad pointed out. "Come on and let's do a sweep."

"I'm with you," Andrew said and followed Conrad through the cabin, checking every room. When they entered the main bedroom, Conrad urged caution and respect.

"After all...the puddles could have just been from Amanda coming in to fetch her gun. She didn't know it had been stolen from the closed box. Let's be cautious."

"I'm with you all the way," Andrew said, stepping into a lovely bedroom fit for a queen. The bedroom smelled of roses and fresh rain, reminding Andrew of a garden after a summer thunderstorm. But this peaceful thought quickly vanished when he spotted Amanda's gun laying on the large king-sized bed covered with a pink and white quilt. "There," he said.

Conrad lowered his gun, walked over to the bed, and looked down at the gun. A note was tucked under the gun. "Got a note," he said and waved Andrew over. Andrew made his way over after checking the closets and finding no one hidden. Conrad picked up Amanda's gun and smelled the barrel. "Gun has recently been fired," he pointed out and handed Andrew the gun.

Andrew took the gun and shoved it inside his right pocket. "What does the note say?" he asked.

Conrad picked up the note. "'I could have killed you. In time I will. But first, you suffer. Let Bertha be a clear warning that I'm in charge.' Well, that's pretty direct and to the point."

Andrew shook his head. "Sounds like we have another crazy on our hands, Conrad."

"Yeah," Conrad said in an uneasy voice. "The note isn't handwritten...looks printed from a laser printer. We won't be able to trace it." Conrad stared at the words of the note and then placed it into his pocket. "I need to call Sarah."

"I'll continue checking around," Andrew said.

"Thanks." Conrad left the bedroom, went back to the kitchen, and phoned Sarah. "Bad news," he said.

"What is it?" Sarah asked.

"We found Amanda's gun in her cabin. It had been broken into, just like you thought."

"And you found a note, too, didn't you?" Sarah asked.

"You'll never stop being a cop, Sarah," Conrad said with an admiring chuckle, looking around the kitchen.

"What did the note say?"

Conrad read Sarah the note. "Someone has it out for Amanda."

Sarah bit down on her lower lip and looked toward the doorway. "Amanda is in the bathroom, Conrad. We need to hurry and talk. I don't want her upset."

"You can't keep this a secret from her."

"I know," Sarah sighed. "But the poor thing is already so scared and upset. That note is only going to make matters worse."

"Amanda is a big girl. I know you want to protect her, but she has to know the truth. She'll have to file a report, a crime did happen in her house, after all."

Sarah closed her eyes and saw Amanda's sweet and beautiful face appear before her eyes. "That woman has saved my life, Conrad. She isn't just there for me in the hour of danger, but...she's there for me emotionally, whenever I have felt...broken. She deserves to be happy...and now she's stuck in a nightmare."

"I love Amanda, too," Conrad told Sarah, "but honey, we need her to be strong right now. We have a killer on the loose and no way of tracking him...or her. Right now, we're blind. We have no evidence and no way of seeing through the storm to find evidence."

"We're sitting ducks," Sarah said in a worried voice. "The killer has the upper hand on us for sure."

"The killer shot Bertha to show Amanda just who is in charge," Conrad told Sarah in a worried voice. "I'm going to call the state police and have them track down that convict who delivered Bertha into town. Maybe someone else was with him?"

"I was going to suggest you do that," Sarah said, "but I know my husband is way ahead of the game."

"Compliments on a stormy night are great if you're writing one of your books, honey, but—"

"In real life, compliments mean nothing until the killer is caught?"

"Exactly," Conrad said.

Sarah fell silent and listened to the storm crying outside. When she spoke, her voice was focused on the killer and nothing else. "We need to find out if Bertha is working with anyone else. I have a hunch she has relatives involved. Get on the horn with London again and give them a good dressing-down. Time isn't on our side. But before you do anything, come back home. I want to get Amanda down to the station for safekeeping. Have Andrew come with you. Amanda can ride with Andrew and I'll ride with you."

Conrad looked down at the puddles of melted snow on the floor. "Whoever this killer is, he is strong. Our Michael is a tough guy, Sarah, and he was knocked out cold. I'm thinking the killer is a man and not a woman. I would suggest the killer is the convict who drove Bertha into town, but I doubt he would be that stupid."

"Could be the killer is connected to the convict?"

"I've considered that," Conrad replied. "Andrew suggested that maybe the killer is after Amanda's husband and using her to punish him?"

Sarah closed her eyes. "I didn't consider that. My goodness, Conrad, there's numerous trails to explore and we're caught in a storm."

"Call London and speak to Amanda's husband. Drill him about anyone he knows. I'll be back to get you within the hour."

"Okay," Sarah said. "Please be careful. The killer is lurking around and could very well be watching Amanda's cabin as we speak."

"I'll keep an eye out," Conrad promised. "I better get moving. I love you."

"I love you, too," Sarah said and reluctantly hung up the phone. A minute later Amanda came walking into the kitchen carrying a kitchen knife. "All clear?"

Amanda blushed. "Better safe than sorry. Even the potty can be dangerous, love," she said and set the kitchen knife down onto the table. "Did I hear you talking to Conrad?"

"Yes, you did," Sarah said, staring into Amanda's worried face. "You better sit down."

"Oh dear," Amanda fretted and quickly sat down. "Okay, love, let me have it...just yank the band-aid off and get it over with...we have to pull the tape off quickly...pull the hair out of the knot and let the pain come...let—"

"I get it, honey," Sarah said in a calm voice. She sat down across from Amanda and picked up the rock the killer had placed in the brown box. "Conrad found your gun sitting on your bed."

"You already knew that would happen," Amanda said in a careful voice and waited for the other shoe to drop.

"The killer left a note tucked under your gun," Sarah continued, keeping her voice even and calm.

"A note?"

Sarah raised her eyebrows. "A note printed from a computer."

"What did the note say?" Amanda asked in a scared voice.

Sarah drew in a deep breath, glanced at the peacefully sleeping Mittens, and then told Amanda what the note said. "Now, don't panic."

"A killer was in my home...stole my gun...killed mean ol' Bertha...and then left a threatening note. What's not to panic over?" Amanda cried. She threw her hands up into the air and then slumped down onto the table, hiding her head in her folded arms. "My hubby is going to have me admitted to a mental institution," she moaned.

"Honey, do you have any idea who this killer is?" Sarah pleaded. "Maybe...maybe Bertha was just an innocent bystander the killer used to get your attention? Maybe Bertha isn't involved at all...or maybe she is. Maybe the convict who drove her into Snow Falls has the answers we need...maybe your hubby has answers," Sarah shook her head. "Sorry, honey, I'm speaking out of frustration instead of thinking like a cop."

Amanda raised her head and looked at Sarah. "Why would my hubby have any answers?" she asked.

"Andrew suggested that it's possible the killer is after your husband and wants to punish you to hurt him?"

"Oh love...do you think that's a possibility?" Amanda gasped. Sarah shrugged her shoulders. "Why, my husband has never harmed a flea. He's the most gentle man I've ever known. I mean, sure, he fusses when he gets an answer wrong on Jeopardy...and he sure knows how to drive me crazy with that bell of his...but he's never harmed a soul in his life." Amanda shook her head. "No, I refuse to believe the killer is after my hubby."

"Now you know how your husband feels when you're in danger," Sarah pointed out. "I never put myself in his shoes before...or in Conrad's. I can't imagine how scared they were when we were being held captive at the hot springs."

"Mighty scared," Amanda suggested. "I guess I never imagined how scared our husbands must have felt. Now that my love may be in danger...goodness, the feeling is quite terrible."

"Yes, it is," Sarah said and looked toward the back door. "Conrad and Andrew will be here soon to take us to the station. That's where you're going to stay until we catch the killer. In the meantime, I need you to call London and get your husband on the phone for me. I have to ask him some questions."

"I was afraid of that," Amanda groaned. She stood up and went to the phone. "Love?"

"Yes, June Bug?" Sarah asked.

"Why is it killers only attack in snowstorms?"

Sarah saw another apparition of the terrifying snowman chewing a peppermint candy cane. *It's not over, Sarah...it's never over. I'll always come for you when it snows.* The hideous words echoed in her head mercilessly. "I don't know," Sarah confessed. "Conrad says it's just a coincidence, but I'm not so sure. The snow seems to change the world into a different place...it's a different story...killers come out and play when the snow falls...they come out in all different shapes and forms."

Amanda looked at the kitchen window. "I love the snow...but right now I'm very scared. In my mind I keep seeing something lurking behind the trees...ready to carry out its threats against me. It could be nothing more than a deranged human, but I can't help but fear something worse...something with fangs, or sharp claws, or bloody red eyes. I know that sounds silly coming from a grown woman, love...but I can't help it."

"Well, it's not too far off base. We have dealt with our share of killers," Sarah explained. "Dealing with homicidal monsters takes its toll on you after a while, June Bug." Sarah picked up her coffee, sniffed the drink that was now only lukewarm, and continued. "Cops have nightmares all the time, and they don't always have realistic ones, either. When I trained to become a homicide detective, I thought I was going to save the world...instead I worked long hours, dealt with monsters, and began having horrible nightmares...dead bodies lying in wet alleys...dead bodies washed up on beaches...dead bodies coming alive to beg for mercy and vengeance..." Sarah shook her head. "Murderers kill in ways that haunt your dreams...in my dreams I sometimes saw myself as one of the dead bodies...strangled, shot...the works."

"I can't imagine," Amanda told Sarah. "You never talk about your old cases, what you saw, the monsters you tracked down. I mean, I know all about the Back Alley Killer because it was in the papers and that monster showed up in person, but...I can't imagine the catalogue of horrors your eyes have seen."

"That's why I write," Sarah spoke before she could catch her tongue. "In my stories I control the horrors. In the real world, evil strikes first and the cops can only play catch-up. And sometimes, June Bug, the killers are never captured. That's the way of it."

Amanda shivered. "Los Angeles, you're not making me feel any better."

"Sorry, honey, that's the life of a cop. A real cop never sleeps easy because he understands the truth." Sarah sipped at her cooling coffee and tried to forget the visions of the snowman grinning at her. "You better get your hubby on the phone. We have a long night ahead of us, and we're going to need all the help we can get."

Out in the snow, far from the well-traveled roads, a man crept into a deserted vacation cabin on an abandoned hillside. He dropped a black hunting bag down onto the hardwood floor and looked around. "This will do just fine," he said and grinned, lopsided and manic. He hummed a tune under his breath as he opened his bag and got to work. "Oh, let it snow, let it snow, let it snow."

CHAPTER FOUR

Amanda rushed out into the storm, her gloved hands shielding her eyes from the pelting ice, and stared at the men perched on two snowmobiles parked in the side yard. Andrew jumped off his snowmobile and struggled through knee-deep snow toward her. "All set?" he asked, reaching Amanda. Amanda hugged her arms around herself and nodded.

Conrad spotted Sarah easing out of the back door with Mittens. "Going to be a tight ride," he shouted over the wind and waited for Mittens to relieve herself in the shelter of a nearby pine tree. When Mittens finished her business, Sarah fought her way through the storm and approached Conrad. "I should have guessed you would want to take Mittens," he called out over the wind.

Sarah stared into a face covered with a black ski mask. She quickly reached out her gloved left hand and lifted the mask so she could kiss Conrad on his cheek. "My hero."

Conrad smiled and patted the backseat. "Hop on, pretty lady, and bring your dog."

Sarah struggled onto the back seat and then helped Mittens climb up on her lap. "Storm is getting worse, if that's possible. And the wind is punishing."

Conrad ripped off his ski mask and handed it to Sarah. "Put this on. Your coat and winter hat won't be enough."

"But—"

"Put it on," Conrad ordered in a loving, stern voice. "I'll live."

Sarah quickly put on the balaclava and then wrapped her left arm around Conrad's waist while holding Mittens with her right arm. The puppy burrowed down into the shelter of her arms and hid from the storm. "We're all set."

Conrad looked over at Andrew. Andrew was ripping off his own ski mask. Conrad watched him hand the mask to Amanda. Amanda shook her head but finally agreed as a powerful gust of icy wind ripped at her ears. "All set?" he yelled. Andrew nodded. "Hold on, honey."

"I'm holding on," Sarah promised. Conrad nodded and got the snowmobile moving into the dark night. The front headlight on the snowmobile fought against the darkness of the storm, barely creating a lighted path. Sarah looked behind her and spotted Andrew pulling out of her yard with Amanda behind him. Her cabin slowly started to fade into the distance, like a ship sinking under a deep sea of snow. Instead of feeling sad, she felt helpless anger rush into her heart. She was sick of fighting killers but felt in her heart that she was caught in a never-ending fight. "Hold on, girl," she told Mittens and hugged the dog with her right arm. Mittens licked Sarah's face and hunkered down on her lap.

Conrad wanted to talk to Sarah, but the wind was too loud. He focused on the road and kept the snowmobile going at a steady pace. As the snowmobile worked through the storm, Conrad glanced to his left and right as they passed different houses along the way. Some cabins were lit up, some were dark, some had smoke coming from their chimneys, and some were warmed by electric heaters. The sight of each cabin sent a cozy feeling into his center. "Wish I were home with my wife, cuddled up in front of a warm fire, drinking coffee..."

As Conrad hungered to be home in front of a warm fire, Sarah searched the storm. She studied each cabin and wondered where the killer was hiding. Even though she longed to be safe at home with her husband, a deadly killer was loose in the storm. Somewhere in Snow Falls a man was lurking, waiting to strike. "You won't hurt my girl," Sarah whispered.

Behind Sarah, on the second snowmobile, Amanda was holding on for dear life. Her heart was racing, and her eyes were searching every dark stand of trees the snowmobile passed. "Don't be scared," she told herself, "you're in good company and no one is going to hurt you."

"Are you okay?" Andrew yelled over the icy winds, keeping the snowmobile steady.

"Scared," Amanda yelled back.

Andrew waved his hand. "I understand."

"I know you do," Amanda sighed and patted Andrew on his shoulder. "You're a good bloke. My hubby thinks well of you."

Andrew didn't hear Amanda's response but knew the woman trusted him. "We're going to protect you, Amanda," he yelled. "Your husband is a good man and I'm not going to let anything happen to you. You have me, Sarah and Conrad to watch your back."

"Who watches your back?" Amanda whispered, and didn't say another word until Andrew pulled the snowmobile up to the front door of the police station. Amanda quickly jumped off and hurried inside.

"She's scared," Sarah told Conrad, helping Mittens down from the snowmobile.

"I know," Conrad said, turning off the snowmobile and

taking the key out of the ignition. "Let's get inside and warm up, okay?"

Sarah looked around and studied the front street. She spotted familiar buildings covered with snow; buildings that held a bakery, a candle shop, an antique shop, a little toy store, a dress shop, a hardware store, a bank, a lawyer's office, a wooden furniture store, and other little stores transformed an otherwise normal small-town street into a cozy home. At the end of the street stood her coffee shop. "Snow Falls has taken over my heart," she confessed to Conrad. "Trouble is everywhere in the world. A person can't keep running from trouble."

Conrad watched Sarah pull the ski mask off, revealing her beautiful face. He watched the heavy falling snow land on her cheeks and nose as the icy winds began pulling tears from her eyes. And for a few seconds, he wondered what life would be like if he lost his new wife. The idea cut through him, painful as a knife. "Let me protect you. I couldn't live without you," he said in a loving voice and pushed a snowflake off Sarah's nose.

Sarah gave Conrad a strange look. "Where did that come from?" she asked.

Conrad took Sarah's hands. "Let's get inside," he smiled and hurried Sarah inside. Andrew followed close behind. Once inside, Conrad walked Sarah and Amanda to his small, cramped office and took off his thick jacket. "Coffee?" he asked.

Amanda searched Conrad's office. The wooden walls were decorated with photos of New York; baseball games, subways, city streets, cabs, beaches and even a photo of some quaint little Italian restaurant. It was as if she had left Alaska and been transported to New York. All she needed to see was some mobster standing out on a street corner eating a slice of pizza and telling her to "Fugeddaboudit." "Nice office, Conrad," she said and plopped down in a brown chair in front of the wooden desk covered with half-read files and several dirty coffee mugs and a messily-folded newspaper.

"I like it," Conrad said. He stuck his head out of his office door and caught Andrew. "I'll keep the girls in my office for a while and then settle them in a cell for the night. See if you can get London on the phone and get us some answers, okay?"

"Will do," Andrew said. "Front of the station is all locked up. I'll have Brent do random foot patrols. Michael and Henry should be back from the hospital shortly."

"Sounds good," Conrad agreed. He closed his office door and watched Sarah and Mittens sit down beside Amanda. "You talk to your husband?" he asked Amanda.

Amanda nodded and took a minute to defrost her chilled fingers before speaking. The office was warm, but she felt very cold inside. "My hubby doesn't have any enemies," she finally spoke and looked Conrad in his eyes. "You met him, Conrad. You know what kind of man he is."

"A bit...stubborn but an all-around good guy," Conrad admitted.

"Stubborn to the bone but so very kind-hearted. Why, my hubby would give you the shirt off his back if you asked him for it," Amanda said. She hugged her arms together and listened to the storm howl outside. "My hubby has never had a negative encounter with anyone...well...maybe a few bad cabbies here and there, and a rude waitress, but nothing serious."

"How about his old man?" Conrad asked.

"Ah," Amanda said and began nodding her head up and down, "that thought crossed my mind. I mentioned that to my dear hubby and got chewed out in return."

"Why?" Conrad asked.

"Conrad," Amanda said, "my husband loves his father. He's a loyal son. In his eyes, that grouchy old Scrooge of a man can't do anything wrong." Amanda shook her head. "To imply my hubby's father might have a hidden foe...oh my goodness, the world must stop."

Conrad sat down on the edge of his desk. "So you hit a dead end?"

"Afraid so," Amanda confessed.

"I don't think Amanda's father-in-law is involved," Sarah cut in. "Not in the way we might think, anyway."

"What theories have you come up with?" Conrad asked his wife.

"I'm not exactly sure," Sarah explained. "I keep wondering why the killer chose Bertha, though. The killer could have easily chosen me or you or even Amanda's husband. Bertha was chosen for a reason." Sarah removed her warm gloves and motioned for Mittens to lay down. Mittens obeyed. "A former felon drove Bertha into town, right?"

"Right," Conrad said.

"How did Bertha even find such a guy?" Sarah asked. "I don't believe it was by chance."

"Me neither," Conrad agreed.

Sarah rubbed her hands together. "The killer gunned Bertha down at the hotel. Now, that leads me to believe two things: either the killer followed Bertha to the hotel, or the killer knew she was going to the hotel. We both know Michael is an expert hunter and a very cautious cop. I can't see him being tailed through the snow without realizing he was being followed. Plus, the killer approached him from behind when he arrived at the hotel." Sarah bit down on her lip. "I'm thinking the killer knew Bertha was going to the hotel."

"I can ask Andrew if the old lady made any phone calls?" Conrad said.

"Hurry," Sarah urged Conrad.

Conrad made tracks out of his office and returned a few minutes later. "Andrew said he didn't see Bertha make any calls. But he did say he left her alone in his office for a few minutes while he talked with Michael out in the hall. She could have called out then."

"Why would Bertha call the killer?" Amanda asked in a confused voice.

"That's a good question," Sarah replied, struggling to form a clear picture in her mind. "Let me walk through it. Your father-in-law helped Bertha...Bertha played your husband like a fiddle...your husband hired her to fly to America and watch you...she arrives in a snowstorm...a convict drives her into town...she gets shot dead by a mysterious killer who seems to be out for revenge...and here we sit." Sarah continued to bite her lip. "Somehow Bertha is the key...but a dead woman can't speak."

"We searched her pocketbook," Conrad explained. "We found a passport, some cash, other typical stuff...you know, cough drops, some hand cream, and a pad of paper with some recipes written down. I'm afraid we didn't find anything that can help us." Conrad sat down behind his desk. "We also found the old lady's wooden cane, but that's it."

Sarah forced her mind to think like a cop.

"Cash...American dollars? Not traveler's checks?" she asked.

"No, afraid not," Conrad answered. "I thought that was strange myself."

"Traveler's checks can be traced," Sarah pointed out. "So we can check that, if the killer took them. But why would the killer steal traveler's checks and not the passport and the cash?"

"Maybe Bertha didn't have any traveler's checks?" Amanda suggested.

Sarah felt confusion strike her mind like a hard rock crashing through a glass window. "It's possible," she admitted.

Conrad folded his arms. "The pocketbook didn't look touched," he said, "but then again, Michael didn't come to for a few minutes."

"The killer could have ended Michael's life," Sarah told Conrad. "But he chose not to. The killer was only after Bertha, which means he wants to keep outsiders away from this sick little game he's playing. It's strictly personal."

"Great," Amanda complained. "I have a stalker. Lovely time for a soap opera in Snow Falls, ladies and gents, come and get your popcorn." Amanda looked at Conrad. "I'll have a hot cocoa if you don't mind."

"All we have is coffee."

Amanda rolled her eyes. "Cops and coffee, go figure," she sighed. "Fine, I'll have a cup of joe."

"I'll go get us some coffee," Sarah said and left the office. She walked out into the main office area, which held three desks behind a wooden rail. The room smelled of coffee and cigar tobacco. "Henry and his cigars," Sarah said and just then, a sudden thought struck her. She rushed to one of the desks and called her old Los Angeles police precinct. "Maybe Pete is smoking one of his own cigars..."

Pete, who was at his desk pulling a night shift, heard the phone ring on his messy desk. He shoved a pile of folders to the side, pushed a fat, half-smoked cigar into the far corner of his mouth, and yanked up the receiver in a fury. "You guys in forensics need to—" he began to yell into the phone.

"I don't work forensics," Sarah smiled.

Pete felt a smile touch his tired lips. "Well, if it isn't my long-lost partner. Where have you been, kiddo?"

"Working on a new book," Sarah explained. "I tried to call you last week, but you were out on a new case."

"Yeah, a bunch of low-lifes are hitting the rich houses in town," Pete complained. "So far they've made off with over two million dollars' worth of jewelry and fine art.

The mayor is breathing down the department's neck...he's a real scumbag."

Sarah grinned. Pete never did like politicians. "You'll catch 'em, Pete."

"I'm not so sure, kiddo," Pete confessed, weary. He leaned forward and chewed on his cigar. "I think we got a few corrupt cops helping out."

"Oh no," Sarah replied in a commiserating voice.

"Tell me about it," Pete replied. "It sickens me. Nothing worse than a bad cop."

"Are you sure some of your guys have turned?"

"Yeah, I'm sure. I've got everything but a warrant. One of the guys is the mayor's nephew. Some hot-shot wanting to make detective. If I drag that bag of alley trash into the light, I'll lose my retirement for sure," Pete explained. "I have to try and track down the rats he's working with and hope they'll squeal like babies when we bring 'em in. Only problem is, I don't have any clues except for a single fingerprint that's pretty smeared. Not sure forensics will be able to do anything with it. I've been waiting on them to call me all night."

Sarah felt Pete's pain. "Sounds like you and I are in the same boat, partner," she told Pete.

Pete took the cigar out of his mouth. "You in trouble again, kiddo?" he asked in a worried voice.

"Not me," Sarah replied, "Amanda. We have a killer in town who is out to get her, and I'm stuck on square one."

Pete put the cigar back in his mouth. "Talk to me, kiddo. Maybe your old partner can help out." Sarah nearly began crying. She loved Pete more than anything. Pete felt the same way about Sarah and for both of them, the phone call was like a lifeline in the middle of a deep, dark, treacherous sea that threatened to drown them.

"I have a friend in London who might be able to help," Pete told Sarah after she had told him the details at length. He tossed his cigar into a round metal ashtray and grabbed a half-eaten box of Chinese food. "We can bypass all the red tape."

Sarah heard Pete slurping up the remains of his favorite Chinese noodles. A tear slipped down her cheek. How she missed her old partner...and even her old life. As much as she cherished her new life in Snow Falls with Conrad and Amanda, a part of her remained in Los Angeles—a part of her would always remain in Los Angeles. In her mind she saw herself as a younger woman, driving in a shiny new cop car down a sunny street lined with palm trees swaying in a hot afternoon breeze. It was a tempting vision. Little details threatened the edges of that beautiful picture the more she thought about it, though. She saw traffic working its way through and around the city, clogging up the highways. She saw the high canyons choked with overgrown weeds, hiding mysterious homes of rich people who did not like to follow the law, and the beaches that harbored strange and familiar songs at all hours of the night. Despite all that, she saw herself sitting in her favorite diner by the beach with Pete, discussing a case. "The good old days," she whispered.

"I heard that," Pete told Sarah. "Your partner knows you miss your old life. All you have to do is say the word and I can get your job back. The department would lay out the red carpet for you."

Sarah glanced at Conrad's closed office door. "A part of me wishes I could, Pete," she confessed, "but another part of me knows...I belong here, now."

Pete shook his head. "I tried to leave but couldn't. Someday you'll come back home, kiddo. Wait and see. In the meantime, let's focus on your case."

"Okay," Sarah replied, grateful to leave her other thoughts behind.

"I'll call my friend in London and get him moving," Pete explained. "I'll have him dig up all that he can on this Bertha lady. He's a retired detective who sits around all the time complaining he has nothing to do but sip tea and read the papers at his local pub. I'm sure he'll be glad to get his hands dirty."

"You're the best, Pete."

"Not until I solve my own case," Pete groaned. "This is a tough case to crack, kiddo. I'm having to wear kid gloves to avoid losing my pension while pounding the streets for answers. Guess I should have retired when I had the chance."

"You'll never retire, Pete."

"No, guess I won't," Pete admitted and gobbled down the last bite of his cold noodles. "Heard you're getting some snow again."

"Storm is pretty bad," Sarah explained.

"I've been watching the weather," Pete said. "It's nice and warm here," he continued and then stopped.

"Pete?"

"What?" Pete asked.

"Your voice went sad. Why?" Sarah asked.

"I went to our diner yesterday, kiddo. Oh, it's still the same, except for a few minor changes," Pete sighed. "I sat in our usual booth..." Pete felt his heart break. "I must be going soft because I started missing you, kiddo."

Sarah felt her own heart ache a little. "You're going to make me start crying."

"Then come home," Pete pleaded. "I have some good

years left. We can be partners again." Pete grabbed his cigar. "Alaska has been nothing but trouble from day one. I mean, for crying out loud, you stubborn mule, you almost died from a deadly virus. You've taken down at least a half dozen killers up there. By now I would have been making tracks back to Los Angeles."

"I can't run from my problems, Pete."

"Problems will find you no matter where you go," Pete barked. He grabbed a box of matches and lit his cigar. "Conrad can get on with the department and you two can be happy here. You can even bring Amanda with you. I like her a lot, she's a doll."

Sarah heard voices. "Pete, I have to go. I'll call you back tomorrow," she whispered.

Pete plopped down behind his desk. "Hit and run, huh, kiddo?"

"You know better."

"Yeah, yeah, I know better," Pete sighed. "Call me tomorrow morning. I'll work the night through for you."

"I...love you, Pete," Sarah said in a quick voice and hung up the phone just as Andrew appeared with Brent.

"Everything okay, Sarah?" Andrew asked.

"Just making a call," Sarah said and waved at a tall, thin man wearing a black coat.

DANGER IN THE SNOW

Brent Johnson waved back at Sarah. "Good to have you on board again," he said in a voice that came out sounding a bit like Bugs Bunny. Why? Sarah didn't know. All she knew was that Brent was a good man, married to a good woman, and he cared about the people of Snow Falls.

"For a while, anyway," Sarah replied. "Coffee?" she asked.

"Just made a fresh pot before you arrived," Brent said and pointed down a short hallway. "You know where the coffee station is. Just make sure to leave some for me." Brent looked at Andrew. "I'll go make my first round."

Andrew handed Brent a powerful rifle. "Shoot first," he ordered in a serious voice.

Brent took the rifle, studied it, and then looked at Sarah. "A cop who hates violence," he said, "my wife sure married a winner."

"Melinda married a good man," Sarah told Brent. "A man who loves violence is a coward."

"Let's hope I'm not a coward," Brent said and slapped a black ski cap down onto his head. "I'll be heading toward the coffee station in a bit."

"I'll save you some," Sarah promised. Brent nodded and bravely walked out into the storm.

"Who were you calling?" Andrew asked. He sat down on the wooden banister and folded his arms. "And why did you make your call out here in the public area instead of inside Conrad's office?" Andrew studied Sarah. "What are you up to?"

Before Sarah could defend herself, the telephone sitting on the desk beside her rang. "I'll answer it," she said and grabbed the phone. "Snow Falls Police Station."

"You must be Sarah Garland," a voice spoke into the phone, deadly serious.

Sarah froze. "Get Conrad on the phone," she whispered to Andrew. Andrew stared at Sarah and then raced off. "Yes, this is Sarah Garland," she spoke into the phone. "Who is calling, please?"

"Do you care who I am?"

Sarah closed her eyes. The voice speaking to her sounded surprisingly young...mid-twenties. She decided to drop the act and go straight for the important question: "What do you have against Amanda?" she asked.

"Everything," the man told Sarah in a voice that sent a chill down her spine.

Sarah braced herself. "Did you kill Bertha?" she asked, hoping to gather as much data as possible before the killer ended the phone call.

"That's a stupid question," the man answered. The sounds of a blazing fire crackled in the background when he paused. "Don't play dumb with me. If you're honest with me, I'll be honest with you."

"Fair enough," Sarah replied. "I guess I need to ask why you killed Bertha?"

"In time," the man said, "you'll get all the answers you need. But for now, I only want to introduce myself."

"Why?" Sarah asked, fearing this was only the start of a terrible game – the kind only a sick killer would desire to play.

"I want Amanda to sweat some," the man said in a simple voice. "I want her to know that I'm around and that I'm in charge. I want her to know that I'm not afraid of her or afraid of anyone in this miserable little town. I want her to know the truth."

"What has Amanda ever done to you?" Sarah demanded in an angry voice.

"It wasn't what she did to me," the man answered, "it was what she did to my mother."

"Your mother is Bertha?"

"In time you'll discover the truth. Cops are good at peeking into closed closets. You cops believe you have the right to violate a person's privacy while protecting your own," the man hissed.

Sarah heard bitterness in the man's voice. "We do what we have to in order to catch the bad guys."

"Sure you do," the man said in a sickeningly sweet voice.

Sarah's mind swirled with questions and she finally latched onto the one she deemed most important. "Why do you want to kill Amanda? Why play this game first?" The question sounded redundant, but Sarah had framed the wording in a way that would allow the killer room to broaden his answer—or so she hoped.

"Amanda deserves to be punished for her crime," the man answered. "The more time we take, the more others will learn of her crime, too. I want her to sweat it out first...suffer through the hours of waiting. And she will, too."

"Amanda is being protected," Sarah informed the man.

The man chuckled to himself. "Nothing a high-powered rifle can't handle," he said. "I could have killed myself a cop tonight. I left him alive as a warning to the other cops in this one-horse town: back off or die. Spread the message."

Sarah bit down on her lip. The killer was using the storm to his advantage. There was nothing she could do except try to lure him out into the open, which wasn't going to be easy. "Cowards hide," she said, deciding to toss an insult into the mix in order to test the temper of her foe.

"Snipers are clever," the man replied in a voice that scared Sarah. "I've killed my share of men, cop. One minute a man is alive...and the next minute he's eating dirt. It's a beautiful thing when you get a clean kill."

"So you're a trained sniper?" Sarah asked.

"I was," the man answered. "Now I'm...independent...for now, at least." The man's mood changed and grew bitter again. "Spread the word, cop, that I mean business. If anyone stands in my way, they die. All I want is Amanda. Once I make her sweat some, I'll carry out a clean kill and move on."

"In your dreams, you pathetic rat," Sarah snapped. "The only one who is going to be running scared is you."

"Is that a challenge?" the man asked. "Do you want to cross my path and become a target, cop?"

"You're my target," Sarah threatened. "You became my target the minute you threatened my friend."

"You're making a very stupid decision."

"We'll see," Sarah replied. "You're not the only one trained to kill."

"A lousy street detective can't outsmart a trained field sniper. You're fighting a losing battle."

"We'll see," Sarah said in a stern voice.

"I guess we will."

Sarah closed her eyes. "Cowards hide. I won't hide from you. Will you hide from me?"

"You'll never see me, cop. All you'll see is death."

"Big words from a coward. Why don't you show me your face?"

"Maybe I will...in time," the man answered and then hesitated. "Will you look at the time...the hour is late. It's time for sleep. I'll be up early. You better rest, cop, because I'm going to make the daylight hours very rough for everyone." And with those words, the man ended the call.

"Conrad!" Sarah yelled.

Conrad came running out of his office. "Couldn't trace the call," he said and kicked the wooden banister. "Who is this guy?"

Sarah saw Amanda creep out of Conrad's office. "We're in serious trouble," she whispered.

Sarah walked over to Amanda and wrapped an arm around her. "We're going to catch this guy, June Bug," she promised.

"How?" Amanda asked as tears began falling from her eyes. "This storm has us blind."

Andrew walked over to Conrad. "Michael could have

been killed tonight. My guys aren't trained for this, Conrad."

"Call Brent in," Conrad ordered Andrew.

Andrew nodded and radioed Brent, but all they heard were crackles over the radio. With a worried look, Andrew ran to the front door and called out into the storm. "Brent, get inside...Brent? Brent!" Andrew yelled. When Brent didn't answer, Andrew stepped out into the storm without any concern for his own safety. A couple of tense minutes later, Conrad breathed a sigh of relief when he returned with a snow-covered Brent, his teeth chattering.

"I'll get the poor guy a cup of coffee," Amanda said and rushed off toward the coffee station.

Brent kicked snow off his boots and began wiping snow off his coat. "I can't see a thing out there," he complained. "The winds are too strong and cut through you like a razor."

"No more patrols," Andrew explained. He pointed at Conrad. "Tell him, Conrad."

"Tell me what?" Brent asked.

"Seems like we have a sniper in town," Conrad told Brent. "From this point forward, everyone stays indoors."

"A sniper?" Brent asked. "I...better go call the wife."

"Use my phone," Andrew told Brent and nodded toward his office.

Sarah watched Brent run off on worried legs. "It's like reliving the same nightmare," she said in an angry voice.

Conrad folded his arms. "I know what you mean, honey," he said and focused on Andrew. "Any suggestions?"

"Stay indoors," Andrew said and ran his hands through his red hair. "And wait...wait until the storm stops and the state police can roll into town."

"I don't think the killer will allow that," Sarah pointed out. "He's going to let Amanda sweat it out tonight but tomorrow...tomorrow he's going to turn up the heat." Sarah rubbed the bridge of her nose. "Amanda is in trouble for something she did to his mother...but I got the feeling Bertha isn't his mother," she said. "Think, Sarah...think," she whispered to herself.

"Maybe Bertha was his...grandmother?" Andrew suggested.

"Why would he kill his own grandmother?" Conrad asked.

Andrew shrugged his shoulders. "Who knows? Just a suggestion."

"Not a bad suggestion," Conrad told Andrew.

Sarah stopped rubbing the bridge of her nose. "Conrad, I

wasn't going to tell you because I know you've asked me to leave Pete out of our troubles...but I called Pete a little while ago."

"Sarah, why did you bother that poor guy?" Conrad moaned.

"Because he's my old partner," Sarah answered, "and I trust him...and need him."

Conrad stared at his wife and saw desperation in her eyes. He backed down out of love. "What did you ask Pete to do?"

"Check out another angle on Bertha," Sarah explained. "It turns out Pete has a retired friend living somewhere in England...a retired detective."

"Sure beats waiting to clear all the red tape," Andrew said to Conrad. "We can use all the outside help we can get."

"I guess we can," Conrad agreed. "If anyone can help us it's Pete."

"Yeah," Andrew said. "I only met the guy a handful of times, but he gave me the impression that he really knows his stuff."

"Pete is the absolute best," Sarah promised. She spotted Amanda returning with a cup of coffee. "Brent went into Andrew's office, honey." Amanda turned left. "Poor thing. She's terrified."

Conrad felt anger boil up behind his eyes. "Sarah, I don't like being bullied," he said and pointed at the phone. "Get Pete back on the phone and tell him his friend needs to put this at the front of the line. We need answers before morning arrives."

"Even if we find out who this guy is...how is that going to help us?" Andrew asked.

"I'm not sure...yet," Sarah said and snatched up a telephone, "but we have all night to come up with a plan. Now, please go get me a cup of coffee while I get Pete on the horn."

As Sarah called Pete, the man known as Connor Barker eased down onto a soft brown couch in the deserted cabin he had broken into and closed his eyes. "When daylight arrives, the game will become more serious," he promised Amanda in his mind, and drifted off into a troubled sleep filled with nightmares.

CHAPTER FIVE

Morning began to break. Weak, pale daylight slowly yawned as thick snow continued to fall, thrown about by a cruel, powerful wind patrolling a scared town. The heavy snow held complete power, paralyzing main roads and streets with wide, white eyes. The little town of Snow Falls sat helpless in the midst of a nightmare – a nightmare that was just beginning.

Inside the small police station Sarah checked her watch. "It's time to call Pete," she whispered to Conrad and pointed at Amanda. "Try not to wake her."

Conrad looked inside a small cell and spotted Amanda curled up on a cot covered with a brown blanket. The poor woman looked cold and scared, even in sleep, and Sarah didn't look much better. "You didn't sleep," he whispered.

Sarah shook her head. "Couldn't," she explained and pulled Conrad back out into the front public area. Brent was at his desk with his head down, resting on his arms. Michael and Henry were standing at the coffee station talking in low voices. Michael spotted Sarah and Conrad and nodded toward Andrew's office. "Still asleep?"

"Off and on," Michael nodded and then rubbed the back of his head.

Sarah looked at the white bandage wrapped around Michael's head. The man was in his early fifties and was in the prime of his strength. Even though he was thin as a rail and sported a comically long mustache, Michael was known to be fierce when the situation called for it – though deep down he was nothing but a gentle family man who enjoyed hunting and fishing. Henry wasn't much different from Michael, just a little shorter and more plump around the waist. Both were good men whom Sarah trusted. She was grateful for their presence as she took in the state of the group. "It's been a long night for everyone."

"You can say that again," Brent said and raised his head. "If I drink one more cup of coffee, I'm going to turn into a coffee bean." Brent raised his right arm and wiped drool away from his mouth. "This waiting is the worst part."

Conrad sat down on the edge of Brent's desk. "All we can do is wait," he said and folded his arms. "Sarah is going to call Pete. Maybe he'll have some answers."

Brent picked up the phone on his desk and handed it to Sarah. "Be my guest," he said and then slowly fished a tobacco pipe out of the top drawer of his desk and clamped it between his teeth. The smell of old cherry tobacco began floating around the air even though it remained unlit.

"Hopefully Pete has some news," Sarah said and quickly dialed Pete. Pete picked up on the second ring. "Hey partner, what's the word?" she asked in a hopeful voice.

"You always did have good timing," Pete grinned and paused to slurp at his coffee. "I just got off the phone with my old friend no more than half an hour ago. I was going to call you, but I had to grab some decaf and a newspaper and hit the head."

"Too much Chinese food?" Sarah joked.

"Doc says I have a heart of a forty-year old, clear as a whistle," Pete explained, "but he says my stomach doesn't like that...what did he call it...oh yeah, that gluten stuff. Bothers my stomach something awful. But I'm not going to live without my Chinese noodles." Pete chawed on the cigar he had popped into his mouth and heaved a sigh.

"I don't imagine you could," Sarah told Pete, feeling a strong love for the man. She could picture him sitting behind his messy desk, feet propped up as he spoke to her. "So...what's the word?"

"The dead woman is the word," Pete said and grabbed a notebook.

"What did you find out, Pete?"

"I found out your friend Bertha has a twin sister," Pete told Sarah.

Sarah had to swallow her disbelief. "A twin sister?"

"Yep," Pete confirmed. "Identical twin, as a matter of fact. I also found out that the dead woman in your neck of the woods isn't this Bertha woman. It's a good thing you faxed me a copy of the woman's prints, kiddo."

"Andrew had our guys take a set of prints before they left the morgue at the hospital," Sarah explained. "He knew the feds would want extra care and attention paid to this, since she's not an American citizen and the embassy might ask questions. Besides, we're not as primitive as you might think, Pete."

Pete grinned. "Maybe not," he said and continued. "The Bertha you're looking for is still in London, locked away in a mental hospital."

"What do you mean?" Sarah asked.

"That woman has been locked away in a mental hospital for many years," Pete explained. "Why? Who knows. My friend couldn't dig up the facts...yet. He's still hard at work."

Sarah rubbed her chin. "What's the name of the twin sister whose body is here, Pete?"

"A woman named Emily Roberson," Pete said and popped his cigar back into his mouth. "Emily Roberson left England a few days ago, purchasing a ticket under her sister's name. That woman wasn't coming to shake hands with Amanda."

"She was coming to kill Amanda," Sarah whispered.

"That's my guess," Pete confirmed. "I have more."

"Let me have it."

"Emily Roberson's middle name is Bertha...Bertha's middle name is Emily...you follow me?" Pete asked.

Sarah nodded. "That's how Emily fooled Amanda's husband."

"Exactly," Pete said. "Emily used her own passport to leave England but because she is her sister's twin and has almost the same name, well, anyone could be fooled." Pete studied the notebook in his hand. "Now here's where things get tedious," he continued. "Bertha, Sarah's old nanny, had a son. When she was admitted to the mental hospital, legal custody of her son went to her sister Emily."

Sarah closed her eyes. She had yet to mention the sniper to Pete. "Got a name, Pete?"

"Connor Barker," Pete said. "The son kept his old man's last name after his folks divorced, which would have been when he was four years old. Court papers state the husband filed for divorce because his wife was mentally unsound...not that the husband was a real winner, either. Records show he got drunk and drowned in a river just last year."

Sarah kept her eyes closed. "What about Connor Barker, Pete?" she asked.

Pete eyed his empty cup of coffee. "Good lad, I guess," he told Sarah. "Served in the British military for a while...went into Special Forces. Records show he's clean. Works as a physical therapist in London. He's not married and has no children."

"No criminal record?"

"Clean as a whistle," Pete reiterated.

Sarah rubbed the bridge of her nose. "Do his records show if he's ever left England?"

Pete scanned the notepad. "Sorry, kiddo, didn't get that far. My friend was gathering all he could in a short amount of time. He gave me a quick analysis and promised to get more in-depth later."

"Pete, find out if Connor Barker is still in England, okay?"

"Your nose detects something bad?" Pete asked.

"I'm afraid so," Sarah confirmed.

Pete chewed on his cigar and fought back a yawn. "You got a dead woman in Alaska and her twin sister locked up in a mental hospital...their father was found drowned...guess we do need to look more carefully at this Connor Barker." Pete tossed his cigar down. "Kiddo, this old man needs some shut-eye. I'll give my friend a call and have him focus on Connor Barker and give you a call back...say...after four or so. I still have my own case to work on...some truly ugly dogs to tame."

"I wish I could help you, Pete."

"You can," Pete said, "by coming home."

"Pete—"

"I'll call you later, kiddo," Pete said gently and hung up.

Sarah sighed and put down the phone. "What did Pete say?" Conrad asked.

"Looks like our sniper is a man named Connor Barker...Bertha's son," Sarah told her husband. "Bertha Roberson isn't our dead woman, though."

"She isn't?" Brent asked.

"Bertha Roberson is in England, locked away in a mental hospital. It was her twin sister, Emily Roberson, that came here and was shot and killed," Sarah explained.

"Twin sister?" Conrad asked.

Sarah bit her lip. "Looks like Emily Roberson traveled to Alaska to do her sister's dirty work...only...Bertha's son shot and killed her. The question is: why?"

Before anyone could answer, a single bullet shattered the front door. "Down!" Conrad yelled. He grabbed Sarah, pulled her down to the floor, and threw his body over hers. "Everyone stay down!"

Andrew, half-asleep and wide-eyed, came crawling out of his office with his gun at the ready. "Is everybody okay?" he yelled. A second bullet answered him. The bullet shattered the front window of the police station. Icy winds and heavy snow began blowing in through the broken glass.

Conrad yanked out his gun, crawled over to the front door, and looked outside. All he saw was a snow-covered white world. "He could be up on the buildings," he told Andrew and began scanning the rooftops across the street. His eyes came up empty.

"What's happening?" a panicked voice yelled.

"Stay down!" Andrew yelled and grabbed Amanda, who had walked out of the cell where she had been sleeping and was very confused. Amanda toppled down to the floor and looked at Conrad. "He's out there, isn't he?" she cried.

Conrad eased away from the door and crawled back to Sarah. "Whoever this guy is, he has the advantage," he said in a quick voice. "Take Amanda back to that cell and keep her there. It's the safest place, it's got cement walls and no exterior windows."

Sarah crawled over to Amanda, grabbed her hand, and then quickly duck-walked back to the cell where Amanda had been resting. "Stay here, June Bug," she begged.

Amanda watched Sarah pull out her gun. "Where are you going?" she asked in a terrified voice.

"The storage room has that small window that faces the street. I'm going to see if I can spot the shooter from there," Sarah explained.

"Then I'm coming with you," Amanda declared.

Sarah heard a third shot shatter Conrad's office window. "I guess you should," she said in desperation, and ran down a short hallway and slid to a stop in front of a closed door leading into a room holding old, dusty items that the department had forgotten about. "Stand guard for me," Sarah begged Amanda and hurried into the room, stepping past piles of boxes. "Just one shot," she begged, finally making it to the small rectangular window.

Amanda watched Sarah step up onto a box, carefully ease the window open just enough to see out, block her face from the wind and snow, and search the outside world. "See anything?" she asked in a desperate but quiet voice.

Sarah gazed around the snow-covered street, searched over the buildings across the street, and looked up onto the rooftops. "Nothing," she said in a miserable voice as a fourth bullet took out the window in Andrew's office. "He's forcing us into a corner..."

Amanda began biting her thumb nail and stared down the hallway. She spotted Andrew and Conrad squatting beside Conrad's office door. "Who is this guy?"

Sarah kept scanning the snow-covered rooftops. The area appeared void of human movement. But suddenly, out of the corner of her eye, she saw a flicker of movement. "There," she whispered, spotting snow fall off the roof covering the hardware store. She aimed her gun at the roof and fired off three shots. The bullets struck the edge of the roof. As they did, a man dressed in a white camouflage outfit stumbled back, revealing a high-powered rifle covered with an arctic white cloth. "Found you," Sarah said and quickly emptied her clip at her target – the only clip she had.

Connor Barker quickly dropped down onto one knee, shocked that his position had been compromised. Fury filled him. "Last mistake I'll ever make," he hissed and retreated to cross to a different rooftop out of sight and establish a new position. Then he began shooting out every window visible in the buildings across the street. When the windows were shot out, he aimed his rifle at a transformer, shot off a single bullet, and killed the power running down the main street. "I'll let the cold settle in before I make my call," he said and melted away into the storm.

Back in the police station, Sarah watched helplessly as the man escaped into the storm. "Come on," she told Amanda, quickly closed the window, and walked at a low crouch back into the front room. "No power."

Amanda shivered all over. It was not cold yet, but it would be very soon. The loss of power made her heart sink. "We're in the dark...again."

Conrad put his arm around Sarah. "He shot up the front street pretty good. I heard at least ten windows get shot out before the power went out."

"Connor Barker wants us in the dark and the cold," Sarah told Conrad. "When night falls, he'll come at us even harder."

"How do you know that?" Andrew insisted.

"Pete said Connor Barker served in the Special Forces...in his country, not ours," Sarah explained. "If he wanted us dead, we would be dead. Right now, he's following through on every word he said."

"What did he say, exactly?" Andrew asked.

"He wants to make Amanda sweat some," Sarah explained, "and crippled us in the process. And unfortunately, that's exactly what he's done." Sarah nodded toward the front door. "We're trapped, powerless and uncertain. Connor Barker could be anywhere, or he could still be right across the street. My guess is he's close, and when night falls, he'll attack again. For now, I think he wanted to let us know who is in charge in order to make Amanda sweat."

"But why?" Amanda demanded. "What did I ever do to this bloke?"

"Not to him...to his mother," Sarah told Amanda and hugged her shoulder. "I called Pete, June Bug, and he told me some interesting news."

"What did Pete tell you?" Amanda asked in a scared voice.

"Honey, the woman your hubby hired to come and babysit you wasn't Bertha," Sarah explained, forcing her voice to remain calm as the icy winds blew snow through the broken windows and front door. "Bertha has – had – an identical twin, named Emily. It was Emily Roberson, Bertha's sister, who flew here to Alaska. Bertha Roberson is still in England, locked away in a mental hospital...and...Connor Barker, the shooter outside, is her son. Connor was adopted by his Aunt Emily when he was quite young."

Amanda's eyes grew wide with fear. "Oh dear," she gasped. "I...I never...oh dear," was all Amanda could manage to say.

Sarah looked at Conrad. "Station your guys at every entrance," she said in a quick voice. "All we can do is sit tight and wait."

Brent crawled over to Andrew with Michael and Henry. "I'll cover the back door," he said.

"Good," Andrew said. "Michael, you cover the basement door and Henry you cover the rear exit. Shoot first and ask questions later. In the meantime, I'm going to start calling everyone in town and order them to stay inside."

Amanda felt her heart sink. "This is all my fault," she whispered and looked at the broken glass at the front of the station and watched the snow pour in. Sarah followed Amanda's eyes but didn't say a word. Instead, she closed her eyes and began to pray.

"A mental hospital, goodness," Amanda said, sitting safe in a cell with a blanket wrapped around her. "I knew the woman was insane, but I never imagined she would end up in a mental hospital."

Sarah helped Mittens up onto the cot Amanda was sitting on. Mittens quickly laid down next to Amanda, looking around as if fully aware of the dangers surrounding her favorite humans. "Pete said her husband filed for divorce because Bertha was showing signs of mental instability. He said Connor Barker was four at the time...which would mean it happened...about the same years Bertha was your nanny."

"I never knew the old bat had a son," Amanda confessed. "I always assumed she had no family." Amanda cradled her arms together under the blanket. The police station was growing colder and colder by the second. The two front offices Andrew and Conrad occupied were quickly filling with snow. The front room was becoming a giant snow drift. A building that had once offered safety was becoming an icy tomb.

"Connor said he wanted you to suffer for what you did to his mother, June Bug," Sarah continued. "That makes me wonder if he blames you for his mother being in a mental hospital. But not just you...maybe his daddy and his aunt? It could be he's finally taking revenge on everyone he thinks is responsible for his mother's mental state."

"But I didn't do anything to Bertha...that old bat was already a mental case," Amanda told Sarah, hearing anger creep into her scared voice.

Sarah sat down on the edge of the cot and rubbed Mittens' soft ears. "Connor's father was found drowned...and Connor shot and killed his aunt at the hotel...and now he's after you. Somehow you three are connected."

Amanda hugged the blanket. "How, love?" she begged.

"Maybe Pete will tell us when I call him later," Sarah

suggested. "In the meantime, all we can do is sit tight." Sarah studied the sturdy walls of the cell. "You're safe in here, June Bug. No one can harm you."

Amanda let her eyes roam around the small cell. The walls were gray, and the floor was solid concrete. She felt like she was trapped in a tomb – but at least there were no windows. "I guess this awful cell will have to be home for a while," she sighed and then felt her belly growl. "I'm hungry."

"Me too, honey," Sarah confessed. "When this is over, I promise to treat you to a real comfort food feast at the diner."

"I could go for a double cheeseburger and a plate of salty fries right now," Amanda told Sarah and nearly began drooling all over herself. "And then I could go for a strawberry shake."

"June Bug, you're killing me," Sarah said and let out a hungry moan. "I could go for Chinese food...sesame chicken...fried rice..." Sarah sighed. "Thanks a lot, Pete. Now I'm hungry for Chinese food."

"I would give anything to be in Los Angeles right now, basking in the warm sun, shopping, eating at that diner you love so much." Amanda hugged her cold arms. "I can see the blue skies and the palm trees...I can see us driving through the canyons that wind up into the hills high above the city..."

Sarah felt homesickness wash over her. "Pete wants me to move back to Los Angeles and take my old job back," she told Amanda.

Amanda looked at Sarah with worry in her eyes. "And?" she asked, fearing the worst – not that she could blame Sarah for wanting to pack up her bags and leave Snow Falls. The poor woman had suffered nothing but one catastrophe after another after arriving in town. A person could take only so much hardship before abandoning ship.

"Oh, June Bug," Sarah sighed, "sometimes I get so homesick for my old familiar life...I can barely stand it. I miss California sun and everything that made Los Angeles feel like a paradise," Sarah explained. "But I don't miss the crime, the traffic, the pollution, the hate...the violence. My heart is torn between Alaska, a place I want to love and call my new home, and Los Angeles, my hometown that is filled with corrupt politicians, criminals, gangs...the worst mankind has to offer under a sun that shines down on the good and the bad every day."

Amanda listened to Sarah speak and sighed with a heavy heart. "As much as I love my life here in Snow Falls, sometimes thoughts of London are the same for me, love," she said. "In the old days, London was a fine city. Today, London is fancy and cosmopolitan, but it has a dark side, too. It has become a...smelly sewer to me. Oh, I still see my old spots that I adore and I still cherish them...but the people, love, have changed, for the worse...and that change has tainted London." Amanda looked down at Mittens slumbering peacefully on the wooly blanket. "England is still a beautiful country. The countryside is absolutely breathtaking. It's the people, love, that are destroying the world."

Sarah nodded. "There's this street in Los Angeles, downtown, that once housed this old pie shop. All the place served was pie. Pete and I loved to go there...so did my ex-husband." Sarah felt pain sting her heart and slowly pushed it away. "A little old man and woman...the Patricks were their name...they owned the pie shop for years and were known by the whole city. Sweet people, June Bug."

"What happened?"

"Time," Sarah said in a resigned voice. "Mr. Patrick ended up dying and his wife had to move away. She couldn't keep up the business or afford the rent. Pete told me a tattoo parlor took over the pie shop, changed all its vintage glamor into ugly decor." Sarah lowered her eyes. "There was a toy store across the street...a bar occupies the toy store now."

"What a shame," Amanda said in a disgusted voice.

"The old-timers made Los Angeles what it was," Sarah said. "The people of yesterday are all dying away, though, and the world is being ruined by people who have no sense of...what life truly is. The people of today are all about money, power, technology, control, sacrificing their hearts to a world of greed and death. The Patricks were fine, Christian people who understood the old ways. Today it's hard to find a business that respects the old ways. It's all about money and—"

"And change," Amanda added. "Greedy monsters are changing the world into a dark hole, love."

"Yes, they are," Sarah agreed. "And that's why I can never move back to Los Angeles. The city was changing for the worse when I lived there...it's surely not going to get any better." Sarah shook her head. "Pete told me his favorite Chinese restaurant might be forced to close because some developer wants the space for a new medical complex. I know Snow Falls is a small town, June Bug, but at least there's still people like Andrew around...men who care to keep an older way of life alive."

"There's us, too," Amanda promised Sarah. "We're not going to let anyone come in and take over Snow Falls. This is our home and we'll fight for it...better or worse. And that means you can never leave."

Sarah looked at Amanda with loving eyes. "I wasn't planning on leaving, June Bug," she promised. "Snow Falls is my home now. Conrad is my home. You're my home."

"Don't forget about our little O'Mally's" Amanda pointed out. "O'Mally's may not be a huge shopping mall, but it's our store."

"You bet," Sarah actually smiled. "I love going into O'Mally's early in the morning, when the doors first open. I love having the store to myself...shopping round, getting this or that, really looking for nothing but loving everything. The other day I went there and ended up buying a simple bath towel. I sat in the snack bar most of the time reading a book, enjoying the atmosphere. Sure, I wasn't at my little diner beside the beach...I was someplace else that had captured my heart."

"Snow Falls has all of my heart," Amanda confessed. "I can't imagine living anyplace else, love. I admit that I miss my old life in London, but I'm also very attached to my new life in Alaska. Why, if it wasn't for that mental case outside trying to kill me, I would be at O'Mally's right this second...either that or calling Andrew and fussing at him to get the plows moving so I could drive to O'Mally's."

Sarah felt a smile touch her face. "Yes, Andrew has told me you have called him a time or two and ordered him to get the plows moving."

"Nothing stands between a woman and her shopping," Amanda declared and then grew silent. A sad shadow fell over her lovely face.

"June Bug?" Sarah asked in a concerned voice, "what is it?"

A tear dropped from Amanda's eye. "My love for this place might not be enough. It might not be up to me. My hubby may force me to leave Snow Falls," she said. "He warned me that if I got into any more trouble, he would move us back to London." Amanda looked at Sarah. "This will be the straw that breaks the camel's back, love."

"No, it isn't, not yet," Sarah promised. "If your hubby tries to take you away from me I'll...punch him square in the nose."

Amanda wiped at her tear. "I could never go back to London," she told Sarah. "I love my cabin, the woods, the fresh air...and my snow. I couldn't imagine living in one of those suffocating flats again."

"You're not leaving Snow Falls, June Bug."

"I wish I could be as confident, Los Angeles," Amanda replied. "My hubby isn't the type of man who goes back on his word. Also," Amanda added in a hurt voice, "his daddy is pressuring him to relocate to London...and sadly, my son is agreeing."

"But your son loves Fairbanks."

Amanda felt another tear drop from her eye. "My son was offered a good job in London, love. My hubby...really has no reason to stay in Alaska anymore. We moved here to be close to my son. He's leaving, which means we have no reason to stay."

Sarah felt her heart break. "June Bug, why didn't you tell me?" she begged.

"Because I...I told my hubby I would never leave Snow Falls," Amanda explained. She felt more tears leave her hurt eyes. "I can't do it," she continued. "I told my hubby and he agreed that if I stay out of trouble, he would continue living in Snow Falls. Now I'm afraid he'll give me a choice: relocate to London or...divorce him."

"June Bug, your husband would never divorce you over something so trivial. That man...why, you're his entire world." Sarah put her arm around Amanda. "I think you're panicking over nothing."

Amanda gazed out of the cell. "I'm not getting any younger, Los Angeles. I want to grow old in Snow Falls. I'm very happy here...but the day might arrive when I will be forced to make a very difficult choice."

Before Sarah could respond, Conrad appeared with a worried look on his face. "Connor Barker is on the phone. He's demanding to talk to Amanda."

Amanda squeezed Sarah's hand. "Love?" she asked.

"You better talk to him, honey," Sarah told Amanda and helped her stand up. "Right now, we have to stay in the game and see what cards Connor might play. If we refuse to sit at the table and play with him, he might do something drastic to force us back to the game...like begin shooting innocent people."

Amanda drew in a deep breath. "Okay, love," she said, "I'll talk to the monster. After all, Snow Falls is my home, and the people who live here are my neighbors and friends."

"That's my girl," Sarah said and walked Amanda into the front room like she was walking a convicted felon to an electric chair. Outside, the winds howled and the snow continued to flood down from a low, dark gray sky, covering the town of Snow Falls, a silent, white scream trapping everyone inside of a nightmare.

Amanda walked up to Brent's desk and picked up an icy cold phone. "What do you want with me?" she demanded, trying to sound firm and angry instead of terrified to her core.

"I want you to understand what it feels like to suffer mental anguish," Connor told Amanda. He walked over to a chair in the warm cabin and sat down. "I want you to understand what it feels like to suffer before you die."

"Why?" Amanda asked, allowing her voice to show desperation. "What did I ever do to you?"

"Not to me...my mother," Connor stated. He locked his eyes on a raging fire and walked his mind back through time. "Because of you, my mother suffered a mental breakdown. Because of you...I suffered under the hands of a cruel man and a cruel woman."

"What are you talking about? I didn't do anything to Bertha. That woman was already a mental case when my parents hired her to become my nanny."

"Don't you dare speak about my mother that way!" Connor hissed and hit the left arm of the chair with a powerful fist. "My mother was the victim, not you."

Amanda looked at Sarah with worried eyes. "Okay...if you insist on believing a lie."

"I speak the truth," Connor retorted, forcing his temper to cool down. "My mother told me all about you, Amanda. She told me how you were a spoiled child, indulged too much by weak parents. She told me how you told lies about her to your parents. She told me how you hated her, pulled awful tricks on her, hurt her, and eventually got her dismissed." Connor drew in a deep breath and narrowed his eyes. "My mother told me your hatred pushed her mind over the edge. She said you tortured her."

"What a load of cow manure," Amanda exclaimed. "Listen, you basket case, Bertha was the one who tortured me. She would sneak behind my back and tell my parents awful lies. She made my life a living nightmare for many years. Then one day my mother caught her in a lie and dismissed her."

"Don't lie to me," Connor threatened Amanda in a deadly voice. "My mother told me the truth about you." Connor squeezed the phone. "You're the reason she suffered so greatly, and I swore I would take vengeance on everyone who harmed her. Now I'm fulfilling my promise. I killed my mother's husband for divorcing her after you had her dismissed. I killed her sister for her crimes against me when I was growing up, feeding me lies about my mother. About her own sister! And now I'm going to kill you...slowly, just like the last two. I tortured their minds before I killed them. Now it's your turn."

"You're a sick piece of work, aren't you?" Amanda asked, feeling anger suddenly overpower her fear. "You're not after revenge, you're just inflicting pain because you like to hurt people, admit it. There's no revenge here. You just like to kill. You're as sick as your mother was."

"I'm killing because my mother has ordered me to finally carry out vengeance against her enemies," Connor corrected Amanda. "I began with her husband, and I'm going to end with you. It was no coincidence that poor Aunt Emily became a home nurse to a sick old man who despises you, Amanda. Everything has been planned. Now sit tight until tonight and we'll talk some more. And if you try to leave the police station...well, don't. Unless you want to die earlier than planned."

Amanda heard Connor hang up. She dropped the phone in its cradle and looked at Sarah with horrified eyes. "We're dealing with an insane killer," she whispered and watched the snow continue to flood in through the front door. The snow drifts piled up faster and faster, ready to bury anyone who dared to get close. Outside of the police station, scared citizens were locking their doors and grabbing their rifles. A killer was loose in the storm and they had no desire to become his next victim.

CHAPTER SIX

Andrew made a decision. "Alright," he said, standing at the back door, "the killer called us from a landline phone about two hours after he shot up the front street. We all know cell phone service is down. It's been about twenty minutes since Amanda spoke to him. Our guess is the killer is hiding out someplace and he's off the radar for the night." Andrew tapped the wooden back door. "You guys get home to your families."

Brent looked at Michael and Henry with worried eyes. "Andrew, we're not cowards, but our families..."

Andrew put a caring hand on Brent's shoulder. "I know, Brent."

Conrad stepped in. "You guys better hurry. Stay to the back of the station, travel on foot, and hurry."

"This storm is going to be rough to walk in," Michael pointed out, "but what choice do we have? If we move the snowmobiles, the shooter will think we left the station."

Henry looked at Andrew. "You sure you want us to go?"

"No sense in staying," Andrew told his friend. "Now you guys hurry." Before anyone could speak, Andrew forced the back door open. "Hurry, guys." Brent hesitated, then he thought of his wife. He took a deep breath and ran out into the storm. Michael and Henry followed. "Now it's our turn," Andrew yelled over the howling winds. "Let's get to the diner."

Conrad grabbed Sarah's hand. "Let's hope you're right about Connor Barker," he said.

Sarah bit down on her lower lip. "This storm is too powerful for anyone to stay out in it for too long," she said over the winds. "I think Connor Barker is holed up somewhere near town."

"Let's not wait around and find out," Amanda said and pulled Mittens to her. "On the count of three, girl." Mittens barked. "Okay...one...two...three!" Amanda yelled and ran out into the storm. She spotted Brent, Michael and Henry working their way through the back parking area to her left. Amanda turned right and began fighting her way through the snow. Mittens trudged along and then suddenly stopped. "What is it, girl?" Mittens whined, squatted to relieve her bladder against a snowbank, and then let out a happy bark as she continued after the group. "Of all the times," Amanda complained as a blast of icy wind nearly knocked her down. "Come on."

Sarah hurried after Amanda with Conrad at her side. Andrew took up the rear. "We can't go back to the cabin," she said, "we have to stay in town and travel from store to store."

Conrad studied the back street running behind the police station. A row of small houses lined the rear street, and each had smoke rising from its chimney. Each house was home to an elderly man or woman who enjoyed living in town. "I wish we could draw this guy out into the woods and away from town," he said, forcing his legs to walk through knee-deep snow.

"Connor Barker would kill us in a matter of seconds," Sarah replied. "He's a trained sniper, Conrad. We have to stay where he can't see us." Sarah glanced over her shoulder and spotted Andrew working his way through the snow. "We have to split up, hide in the stores, and hope one of us gets a good shot at him. We can't let him corner us in one location."

Conrad knew Sarah was right. He respected his wife as a woman and a cop and valued her experience and opinion. "I don't want you out of my sight," he said over the wind, "but we're not going to catch this guy huddled up in a corner together."

Sarah worried that Connor Barker would never be captured. She worried the deranged man would kill everyone she loved and leave her sobbing in a deep snow drift. In her mind she saw the snowman again, the dreadful apparition chewing on a candy cane. *I'm back, Sarah...oh yes, I'm back...you can never run from me...never.* "Amanda and I will hide in my coffee shop," she said in a shaky voice. "You have to take the hardware store and Andrew can take the wood furniture shop. That will spread us out pretty evenly."

Conrad hurried Sarah to the back door of the diner. Andrew caught up, pulled a set of keys out of his coat pocket, and began fishing through them. He carried spare keys to all the Snow Falls businesses in case of emergencies such as these. "Hurry," Amanda begged, "I'm freezing."

Andrew spotted a key with a white piece of tape wrapped around it. On the tape was the word "Diner." He grabbed the key and shoved it into the back door. "My wife had me label all the keys," he said and quickly opened the back door, "remind me to thank her later."

Amanda hurried through the back door into a cold and dim kitchen that still smelled of meatloaf, pine-scented cleaner and stale coffee. Sarah followed. Conrad paused at the back door, studied the storm, and then entered the kitchen. Andrew quickly closed the back door and locked it. "Okay, let's get some food and get to our stations," he said in a relieved voice. "Sarah, looks like you were right."

Sarah folded her arms and tried to warm herself. "I was expecting to be shot at any second," she admitted. "We took a very risky chance."

"What choice did we have?" Conrad asked. "Let's just be grateful you were right and grab some food before anything else happens."

Amanda looked around the kitchen. "Feels so sad in here," she said in a broken voice. "It's like...all the life that lives in this diner has been chased away into the storm."

Sarah glanced around the kitchen. She looked at the large fry grill, the deep basins of a stainless steel sink, and a door leading into a walk-in cooler. The kitchen also had wooden prep tables, shelves lined with dishes and cups and, lastly, a photo of a smiling man and woman hanging next to the door that led out into the dining area. "The diner will have life again," she promised.

Conrad looked down at the bare hardwood floor and then studied the walls. No windows had been shot out here. The diner was old but homey. Yet the usual cozy feeling he felt every time he came to the diner for lunch or a cup of coffee was now gone; and that upset him. Instead of feeling like a regular customer visiting his favorite café in town, he felt like an intruder. "Let's hurry."

Andrew walked to the refrigerator and opened it. "Okay, we have leftover hamburgers...some soup...pie..." he called out.

"Burgers will be fine," Andrew said and walked over to a wooden table. "I'll leave a note."

Sarah watched Conrad pull a pad and pen from his front pocket and begin writing a note. "I promise to pay double for what we take," she whispered and walked over to Amanda, who was peeking through the kitchen door into the dining area. "See anything?" she asked.

"Our usual booth," Amanda said and closed the kitchen door. "Love, do you really think we're going to trick this bloke?"

"Well," Sarah said and began nibbling on the inside of her cheek, "if our trap works, one of us might get a clear shot at him."

Amanda shoved her hands into the pockets of her coat. "Love, no offense, but I think the trap we set was pretty flimsy. Some chairs decorated to look like a person is sitting there and a wire running down to a smoke grenade across the front door? I'm sorry, love, but I just can't find any confidence in the whole thing."

"The wire is also connected to a high-powered flashlight," Conrad told Amanda. "If Connor Barker trips the wire, he'll activate the smoke grenade, which should make him move back, and the flashlight should kick on and give us a clear, well-lit shot at him." Conrad hoped his voice sounded confident but deep down he knew the trap was pretty flimsy. The chances of Connor Barker actually tripping a hidden wire was...well, near zero.

"Connor Barker told you not to leave the police station, June Bug," Sarah said, taking over for Conrad. "We can't take that chance. He's assuming he has us scared and pinned down. We have to make him think we're still inside the station house."

"Decorating some chairs in front of the door is hardly—"

"Connor will know the chairs are a fake decoy," Sarah explained. "When he sees them...hopefully...he'll realize the station is empty and investigate. It doesn't have to be perfect. It just has to get him to walk inside." Sarah rubbed her gloved hands together. "When he calls the station and no one answers, he'll most likely come to investigate...or maybe not. All we can do is try to stay one step ahead of him."

"I know, love," Amanda moaned, "that's what seems so hopeless. He's already stayed two steps ahead of us the whole time. Oh pooh," Amanda stomped her foot on the floor, "here you three are fighting and here I am being pessimistic. I'm sorry, you guys."

Andrew had pulled the tray of hamburgers out of the refrigerator and was putting them on plates. "You're scared and worried, Amanda. Stop kicking yourself," he said. "My wife is at home ready to call in the army."

"Why can't we get any outside help?" Amanda begged.

"Because we are pinned down by a storm and we have an active sniper on our hands," Conrad explained. "Even if the state police could get into Snow Falls, I would order them to stand down. I'm not going to risk their lives when we don't know where he is."

"You don't have to worry about the state police," Andrew told Conrad. "I made a call right before we took off from the station. This storm has locked down most of the state. Nothing is moving. The airport in Anchorage is at a standstill. No flights in or out. We're catching the worst of the storm, and let me tell you, this storm isn't leaving us anytime soon."

Sarah walked over to Andrew, picked up a hamburger, and handed it to her husband. "Eat," she begged.

Conrad took the burger from Sarah. "Now you."

Sarah grabbed a second burger and walked over to Amanda. "My girl eats before I do."

Amanda stared at Sarah with loving eyes. "You're my girl, too," she said and took the hamburger. "Now it's your turn."

Sarah went back to the tray and handed Andrew a

burger. "Not before this guy eats," she said. "Good men need to keep their strength up."

"So do good women," Andrew said and handed Sarah a burger.

Sarah accepted the food, said a prayer of thanks, and took a bite. The burger was cold and plain but absolutely delicious. "Anyone thirsty?" she asked.

Conrad spotted a soda dispenser. "I'll get us all some soda."

Amanda walked over to Sarah as Conrad hurried to fill four plastic diner cups full of cold soda. Luckily the machine did not depend on electricity to work and dispensed the drinks just fine. "Love, you handed us our food like it might be our last meal," she whispered. "You're really worried, aren't you?"

Andrew took a bite of his food and waited for Sarah to answer. "Connor Barker fought with the British Special Forces," she finally spoke. "He's a trained soldier and a trained killer." Sarah lowered her burger. "The trained soldier side of him makes him very deadly...and when you add that skill to a deranged mind, it doubles the threat. We have a man seeking revenge for his mother...a man who has already killed in cold blood..." Sarah shook her head. "Connor Barker is a man on a mission, and he's not about to walk away a failure."

Andrew quickly gobbled down his burger and grabbed a

second one. "No sense in dying on an empty stomach... but Sarah, if Connor Barker doesn't fall for our trap, and none of us get a clear shot at him, then what?" he asked.

Conrad walked over to Sarah and Amanda and handed them each a cup of soda. "That's a good question," he said.

Andrew took his drink from Conrad and drained it. "Delicious," he said and let out a burp. "My wife has me staying away from sodas but if I'm going to die, I don't see the sense in depriving myself of something I like."

"No one is going to die," Sarah exclaimed. She tossed her burger down on her plate and faced Conrad and Andrew. "We're cops...our job is to fight these snowmen and—"

"Snowmen?" Conrad asked.

"—what?" Sarah asked in a confused voice.

"You said snowmen, honey," Conrad explained in a concerned voice.

"I did?" Sarah asked.

"Yes, you did, love," Amanda whispered and put her hand on Sarah's shoulders. "The nightmares are back, aren't they?"

Sarah turned her head and looked into her best friend's worried eyes. "They never left," she whispered. "The snowman is always around...waiting."

Conrad put down his soda and pulled Sarah into his arms. "Honey, why didn't you tell me?"

"Because as long as I keep the snowman trapped in the pages of my books, I'm safe," Sarah explained, hugging Conrad. "But now the nightmare is loose again, and this time it's after Amanda."

Andrew put down his soda and scratched the back of his head. "Is there something I'm missing?" he asked.

"I'll explain later," Amanda promised. She put her hand on Sarah's shoulder. "Love, what happens if the nightmare doesn't fall for our trap?" she asked.

Sarah closed her eyes. "We stay hidden," she said. "If the snowman can't find us, he can't kill us...and maybe... sooner or later...he'll make a mistake and come face to face with my gun."

Andrew continued to scratch the back of his neck. "Stay hidden...yeah, I guess that's about all we can do. No shame in hiding from a trained sniper."

Conrad looked into Sarah's eyes. "Are you sure you can handle being alone?" he asked in a worried voice. "Maybe we should all stick together, huh?"

"No," Sarah objected, "we need to spread out. If Connor Barker catches us in one building, we'll all die for certain. We need to have our eyes in different locations."

"Okay, honey," Conrad agreed and hugged Sarah.

Sarah tucked her head into Conrad's shoulder and drew in a deep breath. "I can handle the snowman," she promised. "I handled him when the water of that hot spring was burning the virus out of me. I can handle him now."

"I believe you can," Conrad whispered and looked at Andrew. "Okay, Andrew, let's pack some food and get to our stations."

"I'll help Andrew pack the food," Amanda said. She patted Mittens on the head, tossed the dog a burger, and went to work. "If this is my last meal," she whispered, shoving hamburgers into plastic freezer bags, "then at least I get to share my meal with the people I love." Mittens agreed.

Sarah unlocked the back door to her coffee shop and rushed into a small kitchen carrying an armload of food. Amanda followed with Mittens at her side. "Hurry and close the door," Sarah begged.

Amanda let go of Mittens' leash and fought the backdoor shut against the punishing winds. "It's freezing," she said, shivering from head to toe.

"Good thing I purchased that generator," Sarah told Amanda and headed to her office. It was nothing more than a long broom closet, but it held the switch to fire up the generator.

"Oh my, I forgot about that," Amanda gasped. "Please tell me you have a heater in your office, love?"

"Never took it out," Sarah replied and set the food she was holding down on a green table and looked around her kitchen. The sight of the kitchen was familiar and soothing. The floors were still the same old hardwood and the walls their familiar, rustic charm – not much had changed except the front dining room, and that was compliments of Amanda. But even the front dining room had been altered from a logging base camp into a cozy, classic, fifties-style diner that offered nostalgia in a sweet, loving embrace. "Why don't you go turn on the heater...but keep the lights off."

Amanda nodded and ran to the office, found a generator sitting in the far corner, spotted a floor heater attached to the generator, and smiled. "Ah, come to momma," she said and clicked the heater on. The heater made a metal clinking sound and then turned on. Warm, soothing heat began pouring into the office. "Success!" she yelled.

Sarah made her way to the office. "Okay," she said, "we'll keep the office door closed and use it as our warming station. If one of us is out of the office, one of us will stay in the front room and one of us will guard the back door."

"I'll guard the back door," Amanda said in a quick voice. "I want to stay as close to the heater as possible."

Sarah sighed. "I assumed you would, June Bug."

Mittens walked into the office, went to the heater, and laid down. "My kind of dog," Amanda smiled, trying to feel hope instead of despair. She looked at Sarah. "It'll be dark soon."

"I know," Sarah said in a worried voice. She pulled out her gun and checked the clip. "I have three full clips with me," she said, explaining, "The gun Andrew gave you has a full clip and you have two full clips in your pocket. We have to make every bullet count."

Amanda patted the right pocket of her coat with a gloved hand that appeared shaky. "Love, I'll do my best to shoot straight," she promised.

"I know you will," Sarah said and looked back into the kitchen. "I better get into the dining room. We'll leave the food sitting out. The kitchen is colder than a refrigerator anyway."

"Love?" Amanda asked in a quick voice.

"Yes?"

"Life is strange, isn't it?" Amanda asked. "I mean, one minute we're fighting a deadly kid in Oregon and then we're going toe to toe with the Back Alley Killer, then we're nearly dying from a deadly virus and now we're trying to outsmart some...well, some momma's baby who is still tied to a diseased apron string." Amanda shook her head and plopped down in a brown office chair and looked at Sarah's neatly organized desk. "It just seems like yesterday we were focused on nice things like redecorating this lovely café. Then it was on to trying to figure out who killed that poor old man from Los Angeles...and his two sons...oh, they were so sweet...but his daughter sure wasn't."

"Don't forget about the deadly model, the mafia, and the corrupt FBI agent," Sarah added.

"How can I forget?" Amanda said and rolled her eyes. "We've sure had our share of the crazies. And the worst part is, we keep thinking the next one will be our last...but they just keep showing up."

"Crazies keep us detectives in business, June Bug," Sarah tried to joke but failed.

"I'd rather retire."

"Me, too," Sarah agreed. "I better get into the dining room," she said and began to walk away but then stopped and checked her watch. "It's not time to call Pete yet...but he could be in his office. It's worth a shot." Amanda picked up the extension on Sarah's desk and handed it to her. "Thanks."

"Anytime," Amanda smiled and dialed Pete's number for Sarah.

Pete picked up on the second ring. "I'm turning into an insomniac," he complained.

"Your grouchy voice is music to my ears," Sarah promised Pete.

"It better be, because I've had four hours' sleep, kiddo," Pete barked wearily as he grabbed a piece of butterscotch candy and popped it into his mouth. "My friend across the pond woke me up...friends are supposed to let people they care about sleep!"

Sarah fought back a grin. She loved it when Pete was in a grouchy mood. "That's true."

Pete rolled his eyes and sat down behind his messy desk. "Don't patronize me, kiddo, I'm not in the mood."

"Grouch," Sarah smiled and for a second, she forgot all about her troubles. For a second, she imagined herself sitting in Pete's office again, drinking bad coffee and discussing a case. But then the sound of the storm and the fierce chill in her bones brought her back to reality. "What do you have for me, Pete?"

"Bad news," Pete said, "real bad news."

"Let me have it."

Pete grabbed a cup of coffee and took a drink. The coffee mixed well with the butterscotch in his mouth. "Connor Barker was dishonorably discharged from the British military," he told Sarah. "Guy went mental and tried to shoot his commanding officer."

"I thought you said his record was clean?"

"His police record is spotless," Pete confirmed. "His military record is a different story altogether. It was harder to find, but my friend dug it up eventually." Pete leaned back in his old office chair and closed his eyes. "Sarah, Connor Barker served in the Special Forces, as we know... He was a decorated solider...I mean, the works. But then one day he just went mental and tried to shoot an officer. The official report stated that Connor Barker claimed his commanding officer made a rude remark about Barker's mother. Witnesses state that Connor Barker became furious, pulled out his gun, and tried to shoot his commanding officer on the spot. He would have succeeded, too, but his gun jammed." Pete cleared his throat. "Reports state that Connor Barker was already beginning to show signs of mental hardships. He was taken for an evaluation and found to be suffering from Post-Traumatic Stress Syndrome. Funny thing is, his doctor said Connor Barker's post-traumatic stress stemmed from his childhood and not strictly from his time in the military."

"Keep talking, Pete."

"Connor Barker was found guilty of insubordination and released from the military with a dishonorable discharge. It was a military court trial, so he was never tried in a civilian court. He was simply discharged, not sent to prison for attempted murder. He managed to become a physical therapist, got a job, and kept his nose clean. At least, that's how it appears."

"What's the real story?"

"Connor Barker made a whole bunch of trips to America, kiddo," Pete continued.

"Why?"

"To see his half-brother. Turns out Connor Barker's old man remarried after his divorce. He moved to America briefly and married a woman. Unfortunately, he divorced the woman a few years later and returned back to London, but not before leaving a child behind."

Sarah thought of the convict that drove Emily Roberson into Snow Falls and a sinking feeling filled the pit of her stomach. "Pete, is Connor Barker's half-brother named Robbie Nelson?" she asked.

"Now, how did you know that?" Pete asked.

Sarah bit down on her lip. "Pete, did you run Robbie Nelson—"

"Already did," Pete interrupted. "Give me some credit, kiddo."

"Sorry."

"You better be," Pete barked. "Remember, I taught you everything you know."

"Yes, you did, you old grouch."

Pete sighed. "Okay, I'll lighten up some," he promised and moved on. "Robbie Nelson spent time in prison for running drugs. He was released two years ago. Ironically, when this street rat went to prison, Connor Barker stopped making trips to America."

"Are you suggesting that Connor was helping his brother run drugs?" Sarah asked.

"All the way to England," Pete nodded. "You see, kiddo, the mental hospital where Bertha Roberson is being housed isn't your run-of-the-mill asylum. That place is practically a mansion and very costly. My guess is Connor Barker needed some extra cash to keep her there in style. But before we go in that direction, let me tell you a real kicker before I forget."

"What?"

"Connor Barker began working as a physical therapist at the mental hospital his mother is housed in." And then Pete added: "Part-time, not full time."

"He wanted to be near his mother," Sarah said.

"Not only near his mother, but he was assigned to be her physical therapist," Pete explained.

"Pete, Connor Barker is mentally ill," Sarah said in a worried voice. "He admitted to killing his own father and has now admitted to killing his aunt, Emily Roberson. He told Amanda he blames them for his mother's pain and the pain he suffered growing up. He's placing that same blame on Amanda."

Pete could tell Sarah was rubbing the bridge of her nose like she always did when a case was weighing her down. "Kiddo, Connor Barker flew to America just a few days ago. I hate to ask this, but how do you know that he confessed to killing Emily Roberson? It sounds like he's in your neck of the woods. What are you keeping from me?"

"Connor Barker is in Snow Falls, Pete. I'm sorry I didn't tell you. He's already shot up the stores on the main street and took out the power," Sarah confessed. "I'm in my coffee shop right now with Amanda. We're...hiding out....and waiting for Connor Barker to show back up."

"I should have known," Pete said and hit his desk. "Sarah, the next time I see you I'm going to kick one of my size tens into your backside!"

"I know I should have told you, Pete. I didn't want to worry you."

"I'm your old partner, kiddo," Pete yelled, "we're supposed to worry each other." Pete stood up and began pacing back and forth behind his desk, dragging his phone across his desk as he did. "You're snowed in pretty bad, aren't you? Yeah, sure you are. I saw the weather. Nothing north of Washington State is moving."

"We're trapped," Sarah confessed. "Connor Barker has the upper ground. He's a trained sniper, Pete. He...well, we don't stand a chance against him." She explained the issue with the state police and the conditions of the roads as well.

"You bet your bottom dollar you don't stand a chance," Pete agreed. "Barker has killed more men than you can imagine. He is...or he was...a decorated combat soldier before he went mental on his commanding officer." Pete stopped pacing. "Sarah, you're going to have to use your brains on this one. The only way you're going to get this guy is to lure him into some kind of trap."

"I set a flimsy trap at the police station. I doubt it'll work."

Pete snatched up a half-smoked cigar from his desk and tossed it into his mouth. "I need to think," he said. "Call me back in ten minutes and not a second later, is that clear?"

"Clear," Sarah promised and hung up the phone. "Pete needs to think," she told Amanda.

"I heard," Amanda winced. "He seems really upset."

"I can't blame him," Sarah told Amanda. "Pete knows exactly how much of a bad situation this is and why he should be worried." Sarah warmed her hands beside the heater. "But I trust Pete and have a feeling he's going to come up with a plan that's going to save us."

Amanda watched Sarah warm her hands. As she did, a rogue feeling of hope entered her scared heart. The feeling caught her off-guard. "Love, do you really think Pete will think of something?" she asked.

"Back in the old days, Pete was the California State Chess Champion for over ten years in his age division. He could have gone to the national competition level but his work as a detective kept him too busy." Sarah stopped warming her hands and patted Mittens on the head. "Pete approaches each case like it's a chess game...some games are easy to win with brute force and some are extremely difficult and require skill and strategy. But Pete has never lost, and I doubt he's willing to smear his record now." Sarah thought about the difficult case Pete was facing in Los Angeles. "Poor guy is also facing a tough case of his own right now."

Amanda rubbed her gloved hands together. "If we live through this, I want to go visit Pete," she told Sarah. "I want to give him a great big hug and tell him how great he is."

"Me, too," Sarah agreed, and they wandered into the kitchen together. She walked to the table holding the food and looked down at a bag of cold hamburgers. "Pete taught me to play smart, June Bug. I'm trying to play smart, too...it's just that I don't see a way out of this.

Connor Barker has the upper ground and all we can do is try to lure him out into the open. But the guy is a trained soldier...special forces...he's not stupid and he's surely not going to walk into a trap." Sarah shook her head. "I guess the trap we set at the station house was pointless."

"At least you were right about Connor Barker bluffing about watching us," Amanda pointed out. "You suggested he had returned back to his hidey-hole and you were right. And because you were right, we were given enough time to...well...get where we are now and...even get some food."

Sarah kept her eyes on the food. "We managed to move our king out of check...for the time being. But, June Bug, how long can we keep running our players alive around the board before we get trapped?" Sarah lifted her eyes and looked at Amanda. "This man is determined to kill you. He's not going to stop until he does. That means one thing: it's either him or us." Sarah checked her gun. "My husband is out there risking his life and so is Andrew. I'm not going to let some basket case kill them or you." Sarah looked back toward her office. "Pete, I need help, partner. I hope you come up with something good because if you don't, I'm going to have to take desperate measures."

Far away in California, Pete continued to pace around his stuffy office with a cigar shoved in his mouth. "Think, old man," he whispered, "how can we catch this guy?" Pete asked. He cast his eyes around his office, shook his head, and continued to pace. "Let's try to understand the facts we have…Connor Barker wants revenge. He is a soldier who went mental on his—" Suddenly Pete stopped pacing. "Yeah, that's right," he exclaimed. "The guy went mental on his commanding officer for insulting his dear old mother." Pete snapped his fingers. "That's his trigger…and that's going to be the trap that catches him and puts him down."

Back in Alaska, Connor Barker called the police station. When no one answered the call, he put the phone down and grabbed his rifle. "Time for a recon mission," he said and stepped out into the storm.

CHAPTER SEVEN

Pete snatched up his phone and called Sarah. Sarah heard the phone in her office ringing from the kitchen. "That's Pete," she told Amanda in an urgent voice, ran into her office like a woman on fire, and snatched up the phone. "What do you have for me, Pete?"

Pete chewed on his cigar. "Mother," he said in a quick, stern voice.

"Mother?" Sarah asked and gave Amanda a confused look.

"Mother," Pete confirmed. "Kiddo, Connor Barker is sensitive over his mother. Do you follow me?"

Sarah struggled to let her mind catch up to Pete's thinking. "Pete—"

"Think, kiddo!" Pete ordered Sarah. "Shake out the snow in your brain and think!"

Sarah closed her eyes. "Connor Barker is sensitive over his mother...sensitive..." Suddenly a flash of light erupted in Sarah's mind. "Pete, you're a genius!"

Pete spit the cigar he was chewing on down onto his desk. "Kiddo, you have to use Connor Barker's weakness to either catch him or kill him," Pete explained. "The guy tried to kill his commanding officer just because he thought the guy was insulting his mother. Use that knowledge to catch yourself a killer."

Sarah nodded as confidence slowly began to trickle back into her worried heart. "I will, Pete," she promised. "You're my hero."

"You would have figured it out sooner or later," Pete assured Sarah. "You're just rusty, that's all. If you get your butt back to Los Angeles I can sharpen you up." Pete shook his head. "I know that's not going to happen."

"I wish we could go back to the old days, Pete," Sarah told Pete in a pained voice.

"Me, too, kiddo," Pete sighed. "You were...and still are...the best cop around."

"No, Pete, you are," Sarah said and fought back a tear. "I...better go, Pete. I have a killer to catch."

"You sure do, kiddo," Pete said and glanced down at his

cigar. "Out-think this guy...play smart...think smart...be smart. Understand?"

"I understand," Sarah promised and slowly hung up the phone.

"Well?" Amanda asked in an urgent voice. "What did Pete say?"

"Mother."

"Mother?" Amanda asked. "Los Angeles, speak real English to me."

"Connor's mother," Sarah said and walked back into the cold kitchen. "Connor Barker is very sensitive over his mother."

"How is that going to save us?" Amanda asked in a desperate voice.

"We're going to use that as a trap door to catch a killer," Sarah explained and made her way through the kitchen into the front room. "June Bug, do you think I can make it back down to the police station?"

"What for?" Amanda asked in a shocked voice.

Sarah walked to the front door of her coffee shop and cautiously eased it open. She studied the storm with weary eyes. The police station was down the street from the coffee shop. Making her way through the storm would be slow going. Connor Barker could be anywhere.

And, Sarah thought, if Conrad saw her out in the storm, he would surely leave his safe position and go after her. "I guess not," she said and closed the front door. "Bad idea."

Amanda plopped down on the arm of a cozy white armchair and walked her eyes around the dim, cold front room. The café spoke of cozy fifties aesthetic and the kind of place where you could just about hear the voice of a loving housewife speak over your shoulder as you sat there – yet, she thought, the voice of murder was overpowering everything else. "Love?"

"Yes?" Sarah asked.

"Connor Barker loves his mother," Amanda said, hearing her voice become sad. She hugged her arms and looked at Sarah. "I know the guy is a cold-blooded killer, but something made him that way. I don't know what and I never want to find out...but...he's only killed people who he claims has hurt his mother."

Sarah looked at Amanda. "Don't feel sorry for a killer, June Bug," she warned.

"Oh, I'm not feeling sorry for Connor Barker," Amanda promised. "All I'm saying is...in his own twisted way, he loves his mother...he loves Bertha. And, well, if he dies, Bertha will surely crumble into an endless dark hole."

"Bertha is already in a never-ending dark hole," Sarah pointed out. "Whether we kill her son or capture him alive, she's never going to have her son back. The woman is...sick in the mind, June Bug, and so is her son."

"I wish it wasn't that way," Amanda insisted. "If I had only known Bertha was suffering from a mental condition...maybe I could have helped her. I thought the woman was an evil demon who enjoyed making others suffer...she was just hurting in her own way and got lost. It doesn't excuse what she did, but it does make it kinda...sad."

Sarah walked over to Amanda and put a firm hand on her shoulder. "June Bug, Bertha is not just a sad person," she said. "Maybe she didn't do the killing herself, but she approved of them and even encouraged her son to carry out the killings. The woman may be mental, but her mind is a loaded gun." Sarah looked down at the floor for a second. "When a person fills his or her mind with deadly intent, they stop being human and become monsters. While it may be true Connor Barker cares for his mother, he is a monster nonetheless...a monster caring for another monster. Can we really let that stop us?"

"I know you're right, love," Amanda sighed, "I just wish...there was some way to cleanse the wounds of the past in order to save the future. I know that's impossible, though."

"You have a gentle heart, June Bug. You care about people...even your enemies...and that's what makes you so special. Unfortunately, we're in a desperate situation that calls for desperate measures."

Amanda patted Sarah's hand. "You know, I still feel sorry for the kid we encountered in Oregon. I would never admit this to anyone but you, but I do feel sorry for our enemies. I feel sorry for them because they live in a darkness...a darkness of the mind that will never go away. They'll never understand life, beauty, love...the way a rose smells after a rainstorm or the way a snowflake feels on your tongue. They'll never understand the sweet voice of love or the laughter of a good friend or the healing pain of a tear. All they will ever know...and understand...is the darkness consuming their hearts." Amanda stood up. "Connor Barker cares for his mother...and as much as it hurts me to say this...we have to break a mother-son bond, which will create a lot of pain for those who want to harm us. And as much as my enemies want to harm me...I don't want to harm them. I know that doesn't make sense...I guess it never will, love."

"Makes perfect sense," Sarah assured Amanda. "It makes sense because you have love inside of your heart, even toward those who hate you."

"Wish I didn't. I wish I could hate the way my enemies hate me."

"Do you really mean that?" Sarah asked Amanda.

Amanda looked into Sarah's eyes and then shook her

head no. "You know I don't, love," she said and looked around. "Okay, so what's the plan?"

"Wish I knew," Sarah admitted. "I have bait to lure a killer, but I don't know how to set the trap."

"And the bait is...insulting Bertha?" Amanda asked.

Sarah nodded. "We have to make Connor Barker mad enough to come at us. We have to bring him out of hiding," she explained, picturing a shadow perched on a snowy roof inside her mind. "Connor Barker is deadly, June Bug. I spotted him on the roof only because he knocked a little snow loose, not because I actually saw him." Sarah looked down at her hands. "Connor Barker could have waited and shot and killed anyone he wanted to, at any time."

Amanda shivered all over. "Scary, isn't it, to know that someone could kill you...easy as pie?"

Sarah began to agree but she heard the phone in her office ring. "Pete, again?" she asked herself and ran out of the front room. "Pete?" she asked, snatching up the phone in her office.

"No, it's Conrad," Conrad whispered. "I've got bad news."

"What?"

"I just saw our target walk Andrew into the police station at the end of a rifle. He was dressed in a white arctic camouflage suit of some kind," Conrad whispered, hunching down in front of a small window. "I don't know how he caught Andrew."

"Did Andrew...trip the trap?" Sarah asked in a miserable voice.

"No," Conrad replied, keeping his eyes on the snow-filled front street. He grew silent and watched the icy winds rip at the snow in some places and build deep drifts in other places. "Sarah, I'm not sure what to do," he finally spoke. "All we can do is stay hidden...for now."

Sarah bit down on her lower lip and looked at Amanda. "Connor has Andrew. Conrad saw him walk Andrew into the station house at rifle point."

"No," Amanda said in a miserable voice. "The poor guy."

Sarah drew in a deep breath. As she did, an idea struck her mind. "June Bug," she said in a quick voice, "I think I just thought of a way to set the bait."

"How?" Amanda asked and then caught on. "Oh," she said and nervously bit her thumbnail. "What if the bait backfires and he kills Andrew?"

Sarah closed her eyes. "Connor Barker," she whispered, "what are you thinking...what is your plan? Why did you expose yourself?"

"What are you saying, Sarah?" Conrad whispered, keeping his eyes on the front street. Even though he was alone in the store and could not be heard by anyone, the cop in him wouldn't speak above a whisper. Conrad feared if he did – somehow, some way – his voice would cause Andrew to suffer certain death.

"Why did Connor expose himself?" Sarah asked Conrad. "This man is a trained soldier and a trained killer. He's...he must be trying to lure us back to the police station."

"I know," Conrad whispered in an angry voice. "If this guy caught Andrew, he must know we're all hidden...scattered...about somewhere. He'll track us down one by one. I just don't know how he got the best of Andrew." Conrad studied the front street with worried eyes. "Either this guy is really good, or Andrew fell asleep at the wheel."

"Andrew didn't fall asleep."

"I know," Conrad agreed.

"Honey," Sarah told Conrad, "stay where you are," she begged. "I'm going to call the police station. Pete gave me an idea and I want to try to put his idea into action."

"What was Pete's idea?" Conrad asked.

"Connor Barker is very sensitive over his mother. He even tried to kill his commanding officer for insulting his mother," Sarah explained. "If I can get him mad enough...just maybe...we can lure him back out into the open. Blind rage is a deadly enemy."

Conrad glanced over his shoulder at the cold store he was hiding in. "Sarah, if you can do that...if I can get up onto the roof...I might be able to get a clean shot at the guy."

"No," Sarah begged, "stay hidden, honey, please."

"Sarah, I'm a cop—"

"I know you're a cop, honey," Sarah said, "and that's why you have to save Andrew. If I can lure Connor Barker out of the police station..." Sarah squeezed her eyes closed and braced herself, "you have to go out into the storm and rescue Andrew. But please, honey, be careful. I don't want to lose you. I love you."

"I love you, too," Conrad promised Sarah.

Sarah slowly opened her eyes. "I know you do," she whispered and fought back a tear. "I'll...lure Connor Barker over to me, Conrad." Sarah looked at Amanda. "I have June Bug with me and together we'll end this."

"How?" Conrad asked in a strained voice. "Sarah—"

"Honey," Sarah pleaded, "you're just going to have to trust me...as a cop and as your wife. If what Pete said is true, and I believe it is, then we can manipulate Connor Barker's emotions and force him to act outside of his training. Right now, Connor is in control because he's obeying his training. I have to alter his mind so he acts like the killer he is and not the deadly soldier controlling him."

Conrad grew silent again, considered his wife's words, and then – reluctantly – agreed. "You're the writer," he whispered. "You understand the mind of monsters better than I do."

"I wish I didn't," Sarah confessed. She looked at Amanda and then back down at her hands. "Don't leave your position until you see Connor exit the police station."

"I understand."

"Okay," Sarah said and drew in a shaky breath, "let's get to work, Detective...love you."

"Love you, too," Conrad whispered.

Sarah put down the phone with sadness coursing through her body. She took a deep breath and thought about what they needed to do next. "Okay, June Bug, it's time to catch a monster," she said.

"What's the plan?" Amanda asked.

Before Sarah could speak, the phone on her desk rang again. Sarah looked at the phone and then closed her eyes. Connor Barker was calling. "It's him."

"Connor?"

Sarah nodded and answered the call. "Hello Connor," she said, trying to sound calm.

"If you want to see your husband alive, send me the woman," Connor said, holding a gun to Conrad's head.

"He has a heat sensor device, Sarah!" Conrad yelled. "He can see through walls. That's how he's finding us."

"Shut your mouth," Connor yelled and knocked Conrad unconscious with his gun.

"Conrad!" Sarah yelled.

"I move very fast in the snow," Connor warned Sarah. "I can find you at any second. All I want is your friend. You have one hour to send her out into the open. If you refuse, your husband dies, along with his pathetic friend."

Sarah felt panic grip her heart. "Stay calm," she thought, "stay calm."

"I want Amanda out in the open," Connor warned Sarah again. "I won't kill her...yet. But the time has come to make you understand that you are powerless here, so I must increase the pressure." Connor looked down at Conrad with cold eyes. "I'm in control."

"I saw you on the roof," Sarah told Connor. "I emptied a full clip at you. You're not invincible."

"I am now," Connor hissed. "The mistake I made on the roof was inexcusable. I admit that. But that will be the last mistake I make." Connor looked out at the snowy street. "When this storm ends, I will vanish with the snow. I know you're aware of who I am, cop. But when I leave your town, no one will ever know."

Sarah saw a hideous snowman leer at her. "Even if you kill all of us, you'll never make it back to London," she said. "You'll be a wanted man. What's your game?"

Connor kept his eyes on the front street. "A soldier always knows where to hide," he said in a creepy voice. "One hour, cop, or your husband dies. I'll be at the police station. No games," Connor said in a voice that struck Sarah as strange.

Sarah put down the phone and looked at Amanda. But instead of bursting out into tears, anger filled her eyes. "This guy isn't going to win," she whispered and squeezed her hands into two fists as she pictured Connor throwing Conrad onto his shoulder and creeping out into the snow in the form of a deadly snowman chewing a peppermint candy cane.

"Are you sure?" Amanda asked.

Sarah nodded and looked at Mittens. Mittens was sitting up at attention, focused and ready for action. "Connor Barker has a heat-sensing device."

"Explain that to me," Amanda said.

"He cut the power out, June Bug, and turned all the

buildings freezing cold. The only heat sources remaining are heat from either a human or an animal, and that's what his device can detect," Sarah explained. She locked her eyes on Mittens. "I'm going to call the station house and force Connor Barker into a fit of rage."

"But he might kill Conrad and Andrew."

"I don't think so," Sarah disagreed in a careful voice. "If Connor Barker wanted them dead, he would have simply killed them." Sarah looked out into the kitchen. "I didn't realize it before, June Bug, because my mind was elsewhere...out in the storm...I should have realized it."

"Realized what?" Amanda asked.

"Pride and arrogance," Sarah replied. "Every killer has pride, June Bug...and that pride makes them very arrogant. You see, a killer wants to be admired as well as feared. A killer wants the world to know he...or she...is in complete control over the weaklings of the world. Connor is no different. The soldier in him is hard at work but the raw killer in him can't help but to resist a little and show off. Connor Barker wants to show everyone just how clever and deadly he really is...like a kid with a flashy hotrod showing off before winning a drag race."

"Do all cops think like you?" Amanda asked and shook her head. "I'm sure glad you're at the wheel, love, because I would be scared to death to take the chance you're about to."

Sarah rubbed her gloved hands together. "What choice do I have, June Bug? I can't send you out into the storm, and I can't let Connor Barker kill us. Pete gave me a weapon and I have to use it." Sarah stopped rubbing her hands and looked at Amanda. "Connor Barker has been planning his attack for a while. And to be honest, the guy is in complete control. The only chance we have at victory is to manipulate his emotions and force the killer in him to silence the soldier."

"Then what are we waiting for, love?" Amanda asked and picked up the phone. "Let's take Pete's gun and fire it into the air and see what we hit."

"Let's get to work," Sarah said and dialed the police station.

Connor picked up on the third ring. "You have half an hour left," he told Sarah in a deadly voice. "Don't make me come down the street. I'm not in the mood for coffee. I am in the mood to kill your husband if you don't obey me."

Sarah braced herself and then ran into the storm swirling in her mind. "Oh, go whine to your mother," she snapped.

Connor froze. "Excuse me?" he said and looked back toward the cell area where he had Conrad and Andrew handcuffed and gagged. Then he focused back on the icy front room he was standing in and looked at the shattered front door. Snowdrifts had continued to pile in through the broken door and the flimsy decoy was half-covered now.

But Connor had never even seen the trip wire, hidden under the snow. The wire lay untouched, and Connor wasn't aware that it existed. It was mere luck that he had not stepped through it upon entering the building.

"I said, go whine to your mother," Sarah snapped again. "Oh, wait, you can't...because she's locked away in a mental hospital." Sarah drew in a deep breath and stared into the face of a grinning snowman. "Your mother belongs in a crazy house because she's a crazy bat."

"Call her a stuffy muffin," Amanda whispered.

"Your mother is also a stuffy muffin," Sarah added in a quick voice.

Connor narrowed his eyes. "Shut your mouth," he warned Sarah as rage began to seep into his voice.

"Why?" Sarah asked. "You're going to kill all of us anyway, so I might as well speak my mind." Sarah continued to stare into the face of the grinning snowman. The snowman stopped grinning and hissed at her. "Your mother is a basket of soft fruit who deserved to get canned."

"You—"

"Oh, shut up," Sarah snapped. "I don't want to hear your

pathetic excuses about how your poor, dumb mother suffered at the hands of other people."

"My mother did suffer!" Connor yelled and kicked over a desk. "Because of the people who hurt her I was forced to go live with a woman who tormented me. In the end I got my revenge on her..."

"Go cry your lame story to someone who cares," Sarah rudely interrupted, "because I don't want to hear another word. Why? Because the truth is, you're nothing but a sorry excuse for a man and your mother was a sorry excuse for a nanny. So what if you hit hard times in your life, boy? What, do you think you're special or something? Do you think no one suffers but you?"

"Shut your—"

"The truth is your mother is a mental case who enjoyed harming people," Sarah plowed forward. "Maybe she practiced on you, did you ever think about that? Maybe she enjoyed harming you, too. I don't know what happened to cause her to finally snap—"

"You don't know what you're talking about! I put my mother in the mental hospital to protect her!" Connor yelled. "She never would have laid a finger on me. That was only her sick, twisted twin sister who wanted to harm everyone and everything around her. My mother is mentally sound, cop! She just needed to be under protection in that hospital while I killed her enemies. Everything...every action...has been carefully planned!"

Sarah heard the soldier in Connor begin to break as the raw killer in him burst free. "Protect her?" she said, keeping up her pace. "Protect her from her disgusting, criminally dangerous son? Her psychopath offspring? Mental or not," she continued, "your mother is soft in the head and I guess the rotten apple didn't fall too far from the tree."

"You're dead," Connor hissed and kicked over a chair. "I was going to kill you with one shot, but now you've made it personal. You'll suffer before you die. I'll deal with Amanda later. I'm coming for you!"

"I'm so scared," Sarah taunted Connor in a voice that was more brave than she felt. "Looks like your dear old mum failed to teach you any self-control. Oh wait, your dear old mum is a looney who couldn't even teach you how to be normal." Amanda gave Sarah a strange look. Sarah shrugged her shoulders. "I'm trying my best. I've never been good at insults," she whispered. Amanda grinned and gave her a thumbs up.

"I'm going to make you eat your words!" Connor screamed as his rage finally took full control and forced the soldier inside of his mind to cower down in a dark corner. The vicious killer crawled out of a hidden closet in his mind and took full control. "I'm going to...I'm going to—"

"To kill me, yeah, yeah," Sarah said. "Save it, crybaby," she insulted Connor. "I've heard it all before. I can't tell you how many times a deranged idiot like yourself has threatened to kill me. Why don't you go cry to your pathetic, creepy...smelly mother?"

"Smelly?" Amanda asked in a whisper.

Sarah shrugged her shoulders again. "Did you hear me, kid?"

Connor's eyes began dripping with hot tears that burned him like snake venom. "You're going to die a very slow and painful death, cop." Connor grabbed his rifle. "Mother asked me to be cruel, but the army taught me to kill with one shot. I believe in mercy killings. I drowned my old man very quickly and shot my aunt dead without causing her any pain...even though she deserved to suffer." Connor looked at the shattered front door. "Mother made me promise to torture Amanda more than anyone else. Amanda was the one person I couldn't grant mercy. But now, cop," he hissed, "you're going to take her place. I'm going to teach you what real pain is. And while you suffer, I'll make you watch as I put a bullet in your friend and end her miserable life."

"You're really pathetic," Sarah told him. "You actually think I care about who you killed in the past? I worked as a homicide detective on the streets of Los Angeles for years. I've grown numb to that kind of detail. I couldn't care less who you kill. All I care about is smearing your face into the snow and embarrassing your mother. No one comes to my town and threatens me." Sarah felt like a young high school kid telling another kid it was time to punch it out. "Don't forget, I caught the Back Alley Killer. You're nothing compared to him...and neither is your stupid idiot of a lunatic mother."

Sarah's words cemented the killer in place. The trained soldier in Connor completely vanished from his insane mind. "I'm coming for you."

"Come on down," Sarah taunted Connor. "I'll be waiting for you."

"Will you?" Connor asked as a vicious grin struck his face. "You aren't trying to play games with me, cop?"

"No games," Sarah said. "Show me your stuff, punk."

Connor's grin widened as complete insanity took over his raging heart. "I will," he promised and slammed down the phone.

Sarah quickly hung up and looked at Amanda. "Okay, June Bug, Connor Barker is on his way. Your job is to get out into the storm and—"

"And go free Conrad and Andrew," Amanda finished for Sarah. "I assumed that was the plan," she said. "And I'm to take Mittens with me."

Sarah nodded. She tried to control the shaking in her hands. "I'm confident Connor is going to scan the coffee shop with his heat device," she said and pointed at the heater and the solar generator. "Those two items will look like heat sources, which I'm hoping will trick Connor Barker into believing we're inside. In the meantime, I'm going to hide out in the snow...bury myself in a drift, and wait until he enters the coffee shop." Sarah hurried Amanda and Mittens to the back door. "When Connor finds out he's been tricked, he'll move back outside and—"

"And you'll shoot him," Amanda said.

"If I can get a clean shot," Sarah admitted.

Amanda stared at the back door and listened to the storm howl outside. "How do I get to the station, love? I can't very well just walk up the street like I'm off on a picnic."

"Go to the end of the alley, cut down Snow Owl Lane, make a wide loop, and then circle back around and come up Polar Cane Drive," Sarah explained.

"That's a really wide circle," Amanda said. "It'll take me a good half hour to make that kind of distance in this storm, love. The snow is up to our knees and getting deeper by the minute."

"June Bug," Sarah said and put her hands on Amanda's shoulders, "if my plan fails and Connor kills me, he'll start searching for you. He'll realize you're not here, almost immediately. If I can't take him out and he starts to follow your tracks...this will give you a little head start and maybe enough time to reach the station and free Conrad and Andrew."

"Don't talk like that," Amanda begged and hugged Sarah. "You're not going to die, do you hear me? We're going to grow old together and become two crabby old ladies fussing about how O'Mally's never gives proper discounts."

Sarah felt a tear sting her eye. "I pray you're right," she whispered and looked at Amanda. "You know, Pete keeps hounding me to move back to Los Angeles and pick up my badge again. I left Los Angeles after my husband divorced me in order to get away from everything that destroyed my marriage...but now, here I am, trapped in everything I was running from." Sarah scanned the cold kitchen and focused back on Amanda. "I've been trying to run from myself, June Bug...from the snowman. But now it's time to fight. Maybe Connor Barker will kill me...maybe he won't. But if I don't fight the snowman...the snowman will continue to haunt me."

Amanda looked deep into Sarah's eyes and saw a scared woman but a very brave cop. "I know why Pete wants you back, love," she whispered. "You're really something special."

"No," Sarah objected, "I'm nothing special. I'm only a woman who is tired of being scared."

"That's not true," Amanda said. "You once told me it was

Pete who helped you capture the Back Alley Killer. And maybe Pete did help out some, but it was you, love, who went after that savage animal."

"And in return," Sarah confessed, "the snowman came to life. Each case...each murder...represented a snowflake that slowly began to build the snowman." Sarah put her hand on the doorknob. "We all have our own monsters to face, honey...for better or worse."

Amanda hugged Sarah. "Because you've never stopped fighting your monster, love, a lot of people are very safe tonight."

"Tell me that after I threaten your hubby if he tries to take you away from me," Sarah whispered and opened the back door. "Hurry," she begged.

Amanda looked out into the storm as the icy winds crawled into the kitchen and began grabbing at her face. "What do I do if I reach the station and manage to free Conrad and Andrew?" she asked in a scared voice.

"It should be all over by then," Sarah explained. "If it isn't...Connor will try to kill you. All you can do is fight back with everything you've got." Sarah walked Amanda out into the stormy alley and looked up into a low, dark gray sky flooded with powerful snow. "Hurry," she urged Amanda.

Amanda hesitated, looked up and down the alley, made a pained face, and then ran off with Mittens. Mittens looked back at Sarah and let out a low whine. "Love you too, girl," Sarah whispered and quickly closed the back door, looked around, spotted a deep snow drift, and began burying her body in the cold snow. Five minutes later, a dark figure appeared in the alley carrying a deadly rifle and a black hand-held device that looked like a scanner. The figure eased up to the back door, aimed the device ahead of him, and stood very still.

"Very good," Connor grinned, reading the heat sources coming from Sarah's office. If the soldier in him had been in charge, Connor would have realized that one heat source was stronger than the other and that both heat sources were not transmitting human body heat. But because the killer in him was in full control, filled with murderous rage and hungry for vengeance, Connor saw the heat signature on the screen and simply allowed his rage to consume him: he needed to reach Sarah and Amanda. "Now it's time to play," he said, and without any hesitation, he threw down the device in his hand, prepared his rifle, kicked open the back door, and charged into the coffee shop like a wild animal entering a den full of chickens.

Sarah eased her head out of the snowdrift she was buried in, brought out her gun, aimed it at the back door, and waited for Connor to return outside. "Okay, snowman," she whispered in a trembling voice, "it's time to die." *I'll never die,* the snowman hissed at Sarah and began laughing insanely. *I'll never die...I'll never die...never die...*

CHAPTER EIGHT

What had begun as a funny dilemma for Amanda – the return of an old nanny – was now about to end with Sarah fighting a nightmare within her own heart. Instead of battling a mean old British nanny, intent on driving Amanda insane, Sarah was now tucked inside a freezing snow drift waiting to get a clean shot at a vicious killer, hoping to conclude a very serious game without any further deaths. "Come on," she whispered through chattering teeth, feeling her body turning into an iceberg, "step outside...just one shot..."

Connor Barker didn't hear Sarah. He was standing in Sarah's office looking at a heater and solar generator with fury in his eyes. "No!" he yelled and kicked Sarah's desk so hard the desk toppled over, hit the heater, and unplugged it from the solar generator. "No!" Connor spun around and ran out of the office, searched the kitchen, threw his eyes at the back door, and aimed his body back toward the storm, not knowing that Sarah was outside in the alley, hidden in a snowdrift, with her gun at the ready. "Where are you?" he hissed, stepping out into the storm. As soon as his white boots hit the snowy alley, he saw a man shoving a woman forward in the distance. "Ah," he grinned. "Right on time."

Sarah saw Connor step out of the back door of the diner and realized she had a perfect, clear shot at him. She held her breath and began to squeeze the trigger, then saw his eyes dart to the right. She followed his gaze. "No," she whispered, spotting a cruel man shoving Amanda forward through the snow.

"Look what I caught!" Robbie Nelson yelled at Connor. He pushed Amanda up to Connor. "Caught this lady trying to escape."

Amanda yanked her arm away from Robbie and threw a defiant look at the face of the man in front of her, who still wore a white camouflage ski mask. "Show me your face," she demanded in a hard voice even though her heart was shaking in fear.

Connor grinned, raised his left hand, and removed the ski mask. "Here I am," he told Amanda.

Amanda froze. "You're...a monster," she whispered.

Connor ran his left hand over a face that held no trace of

a soul or a heart – the face of a dead man walking the earth in the form of a monster. "Where is your friend?" he asked Amanda as the snow and winds attacked his face.

Amanda tried to step away from Connor, but Robbie shoved her forward. "Leave me alone!" she yelled.

Sarah aimed her gun at Robbie. She couldn't see the man's face because he was wearing a black ski mask, but she could easily make out his form against the pale snow. "Step to the right, June Bug," she begged in a whisper. "If I fire from this angle and miss, I might hit you."

"What do you want to do with her?" Robbie asked Connor.

Connor slid his ski mask back on. "I'll deal with her later," he said and studied the alley, standing in a way that blocked Sarah from getting a clear shot at him. "Come on." Connor grabbed Amanda's arm, pulling her back into the coffee shop. He waited for Robbie to follow and slammed the back door closed. "Take her out the front and lock her in the police station with the other two."

Robbie pointed an ugly black gun at Amanda, and ordered her to move. "Out front," he said.

"Before I leave," Amanda said and locked eyes with Connor, "I want to speak my piece."

"Shut up, you—"

"You shut up and listen to me!" Amanda yelled. "Regardless of what happened to you in the past, it doesn't give you the right to harm people. Revenge is a cowardly act, do you hear me? And don't start telling me about your mother, either. Bertha may or may not have mental issues, but I do know she has a mean spirit to her...a heart without love or compassion for mankind."

"Shut up—"

Amanda raised her hand and slapped Connor across his face before he could stop her. "Kill me if you want," she said, "but you're going to hear the truth."

"Want me to shoot her?" Robbie asked.

Connor stared at Amanda and then slowly shook his head no. "I promised my mother this one would suffer. Take her to the police station and lock her up. If the other two try anything, shoot them."

"You're a coward," Amanda told Connor in a sickened voice.

"A coward?" Connor asked. He grabbed Amanda's wrist. "Lady, my old man had my mother put away in a mental hospital against her will and then he divorced her. I was forced to go live with a woman that abused me, starved me, and beat me with sticks...a woman that murdered what little hope I had left in my heart. I could deal with that because I knew someday I was going to kill her. My focus was on the person who pushed my mother over the edge, and that person was you. All my mother ever talked about was you." Connor narrowed his eyes. "She hated my old man and she hated her sister and ordered me to kill them, but she made me promise to punish you."

"You don't—"

"Listen to me," Connor snapped. "My mother isn't mentally ill," he continued, "she's a hard woman, that's all. You were simply a spoiled brat who couldn't handle normal discipline, did you ever consider that? When you had her dismissed from her position, your mother spoke ill of her all around town and she couldn't find work. No one in London would hire her because of the black mark on her record." Connor squeezed Amanda's wrist painfully in his grip.

"You're hurting me."

"Shut up!" Connor yelled. "You're the one that's going to hear the truth." Connor glanced at Robbie and then back at Amanda. "My mother began drinking her sorrows away. She became...difficult to deal with. My old man couldn't deal with her anymore and had her locked away in a mental home that wasn't fit for a rat! She spent many years in that hovel." Connor's eyes began dripping with venom. "After being released, she found me. I was in the military at the time. My mother came to me and begged me to take revenge. To kill everyone who harmed her. It was the least I could do for the woman who sacrificed so much for me."

"I don't care," Amanda promised Connor. "It doesn't change the fact that it's wrong!"

Connor ignored Amanda and walked his mind back through time. He saw himself standing in a lonely room with the woman who begged him to use his military-trained killing skills to punish Amanda. "I want you to kill your father, too," Bertha spoke in a cold voice as a hard, London rain fell outside the filthy window. "I want you to kill him for betraying me."

Connor stared into his mother's eyes and saw tears streaming down her face, though not a trace of sadness was anywhere in her expression. "I'm confused, I don't—"

"They hurt me, Connor," Bertha cried and grabbed the old, worn-down, brown dress covering her skinny frame. "They locked me away in a prison and now I'm forced to beg for food." Bertha wiped at her fake tears and grabbed her tangled, ratty gray hair. "Look at me, son...look what they did to me. Look what I survived to come back to you. I need you. I need you to do this, my son, my only boy. Don't you see?"

Connor stared at his mother. As he did, his heart began to hear her plea and fill with anger. "I always dreamed of getting revenge on Aunt Emily for what she did to me," he confessed. "It would feel good to kill her..."

Bertha walked across a dirty wooden floor and wrapped her skeletal arms around Connor. "You can kill my sister," she promised. "But first I need her. I need your daddy, too. Let them live until I get what I need from them, and then kill them. But there's one, Connor...one very special person from my past that I want you to kill very slowly." Bertha looked up into Connor's eyes. "I have a plan, son. If you listen to your mother, everything will be okay."

"A plan?" Connor asked.

"You're going to do everything exactly the way I say. You'll get me readmitted to a mental hospital...a nicer one this time. That way no one can throw suspicion on me. And then I want you to fly to America and find your half-brother. We're going to need money and he is involved with drugs. I also want you to leave the military. I want you to get a job at the mental hospital that's going to become my new home." A soulless grin slithered across Bertha's face as she showed Connor her black teeth. "We're going to be very careful, son, and very clever in carrying out justice." And with those words, Bertha slowly began to reveal her plan to Connor, forcing his already-unstable heart to harden into that of a deadly killer.

"You see," Connor told Amanda and let go of her wrist, "the guilty must be punished."

Amanda closed her eyes, tried to think, and looked at

Connor. "Okay, sure, you slimy bloke, maybe your aunt deserved a few good slaps across the face for hurting you...but killing people? That's going too far."

"Death must come to those who do harm," Connor promised Amanda and nodded at Robbie. "Get her out of here. I have to go track down a missing rat."

"Let's go," Robbie ordered Amanda.

Amanda hesitated. Robbie had found the gun she had hidden in her coat. She was helpless to do anything... except buy time. Sarah was outside buried in a snowdrift. Surely, Amanda hoped, her best friend would appear at any minute. She needed to delay the two men. But how? It was clear that Connor was through talking to her. So Amanda did what any woman in her situation might do. She feigned a panic attack.

"You can't kill me! I have a family, you evil man. Oh, my...I don't feel so good..." she said, and she fell down in a heap, pretending to faint. "I hope this works," she thought, lying on the kitchen floor with her eyes closed. "Sarah, honey, hurry and do something."

"Oh, what now?" Robbie complained. He bent down and studied Amanda's face. "We don't need this. Should I just kill her here?"

Connor stood over Amanda like a dark tower. "No, not yet. Pick her up and carry her out of here if you have to," he ordered Robbie. "I have work to do."

"I should charge you more money," Robbie told Connor in a voice that didn't sit well with his half-brother.

Connor grabbed Robbie up by his shoulder and threw him across the kitchen. Robbie crashed into a table and toppled down onto the floor. "What was that for?" he asked.

"Don't you ever speak out of turn," Connor yelled at Robbie, turning his back to Amanda.

Robbie locked his eyes on the rifle Connor was holding in his right hand. Fear filled his heart. "I'm sorry," he said, crawling up onto his knees. "What's your problem, man? I was only...kidding around, you know? Take it easy."

Connor raised his rifle and aimed it straight at Robbie. "I don't like jokes," he warned.

"Hey...what are you doing?" Robbie yelled. "We're brothers...right?"

"I don't have a brother," Connor told Robbie, staring into a pair of terrified eyes. "If you ever talk out of line again, I'll take you down without hesitation. You'll bleed in the snow like a deer torn open by a bear, is that clear?"

"Yeah...yeah, we're clear," Robbie promised in a shaky voice.

Amanda peeked open her eyes, spotted Connor standing with his back to her, and then glanced toward the back door. The doorknob on the back door was slowly turning. "Oh my," Amanda thought as panic struck her chest.

Outside in the storm, Sarah was slowly turning the doorknob. Her plan was to burst into the kitchen and take her foes by surprise. But then she stopped turning the doorknob and lowered her eyes down at the snow. "Not smart," she said, "you're acting in desperation because you're scared for Amanda. Now think...think..."

Sarah bit down on her lower lip and then looked down the long, storm-chilled alley. A shadowy four-legged figure was running toward her. "Mittens," she whispered. "Oh, Mittens." Mittens ran to Sarah and began jumping on her. "Oh girl, you're safe," Sarah said in a relieved voice. Mittens, worried by the dangers in the storm, let out a low bark and licked Sarah's gloved hand. Sarah quickly pulled Mittens behind a wooden trash bin enclosure and squatted down. "They have Amanda, girl," she said, staring at the back door. "I need a plan." Mittens stared at Sarah with sad eyes. Mittens didn't have a plan to offer. "I know, girl," Sarah said. "If I try and make it to the station and let Conrad and Andrew free, Connor might kill Amanda..."

Sarah leaned her head against the wood surface. "Connor Barker has that heat device..." she said in a worried voice. "He'll surely scan the station house before entering...if his scan comes up cold...too risky," she told Mittens. "I have to leave Conrad and Andrew in place for Amanda's

DANGER IN THE SNOW

sake." Sarah listened to the icy winds. "We have a hostage situation on our hands, Mittens. And unfortunately, I pushed the killer over the edge...oh, why didn't I focus more on his brother? Stupid...stupid..."

Mittens let out a low whine and licked Sarah's hand again. "Thanks, girl," Sarah sighed and straightened up her head. As she did, an idea struck her mind. She quickly touched the wooden trash bin and then looked at Mittens. "Maybe...it could work," she said. "Mittens, baby, momma is going to need your help." Mittens stared at Sarah and watched her owner remove a snow-covered lid off the trash bin holder. "Okay, girl, here's the plan. I need you to get inside this bin and act as a source of heat." Mittens looked at the trash can, shook snow off her fur, and let out a miserable whine. "I know, girl, tough times call for desperate actions. We're facing a deadly killer." Sarah ran her gloved hands over Mittens' scared head. "We have to out-think our opponent, girl...two opponents, now. We have to be very clever and very smart." Sarah saw Pete's face enter her worried mind. "Think smart...be smart, kiddo," she heard Pete whisper into her ear. "Okay, Pete, I'll think smart and be smart." Sarah looked into the bin. The trash containers, luckily, were empty. "Okay, girl," she said and gently wrapped her arms around Mittens, "let's get you out of the snow for a while."

As Sarah placed Mittens into the trash can, Amanda listened to Connor continue to terrorize his half-brother, overwhelmed with confusion. "Why did you stop?" she whispered, wondering why Sarah backed away from storming into the kitchen. "Where are you, love?"

"Get to your feet and take that woman to the police station and lock her up," Connor snapped at Robbie without lowering his gun. "If you step out of line again, I'll do worse than kill you. I'll make a call."

"A call?" Robbie asked.

"I know where all your drugs are stashed in your home," Connor grinned. "All I have to do is make one call and it's back to prison for you."

"No...please," Robbie begged, "I can't...I can't go back to prison. Anything but prison, Connor."

Connor lowered his rifle. "My mother is covering my rear position," he warned. "If you try and betray me, she'll make the call and tell them where to look. Now do as I say."

"Okay, okay," Robbie said, scrambled to his feet, and ran over to Amanda. "Maybe I make her walk?" he asked.

"Just pick her up and carry her out of here!" Connor yelled.

Robbie wasn't so sure he could pick up Amanda. Unlike Connor, he was a small man who wasn't very strong. Years of drug use had drained his mind and strength. But what choice did he have? He bent down, grabbed Amanda, and with great difficulty, lugged her over his shoulder and stumbled out of the kitchen. He began making his way out into the storm, unaware that he was going to set off a hidden trip wire at the police station.

As soon as Robbie stepped out into the storm, Sarah began throwing snowballs at the back door. "Come out and play," she whispered and waited for a monster to appear.

Connor turned around furiously at the sudden flurry of noise and aimed his rifle at the back door and listened. *Thud...thump...thud...thump.* Listening closely, it was clear that it was snow hitting the door, from the way the snowballs fell into pieces and made a little sound as they fell down after each strike. One snowball after another struck the back door. The soldier in Connor cried out from a far and distant place, crying out for caution. The disciplined soldier begged to be called out of hiding, but the killer that was controlling Connor's mind ignored the voice of caution and sneered at the back door, heading out into the storm.

"Come out," Sarah begged. She threw one more snowball and then ran to the end of the alley and hid behind the edge of a building. Seconds later, the back door to the coffee shop burst open. Connor stepped out into the snow with his rifle in his right hand and the infrared scanner in his left hand.

"Where are you?" Connor whispered and began scanning the alley with the heat device. When the device locked onto the heat of an object hidden in a snow drift, he grinned. "Ah, so you're hiding over there," he said and threw the device down. It fell into knee-deep snow and he eased over to the trash container covered in a snow drift, looking like a monster crawling out of a dark closet. "I know you're hiding in the drift," he yelled and aimed his rifle at the center of the pile of snow. Poor Mittens let out a whine and hunkered down. "Come out before I begin firing!"

Sarah watched a monster dressed in white arctic camouflage aim a deadly high-powered rifle at her poor dog. She aimed her gun at him and carefully lined up a clear shot. "Time to die, snowman," she said, and without wasting another second, fired her gun. Only, her gun didn't fire. The snow and cold had caused the gun to jam. "No," Sarah said and began banging the barrel of her gun against her leg. "Not now...not again."

Connor, unaware that Sarah's gun had jammed on her, began to pull the trigger but then quickly stopped himself. "No, not yet," he grinned. Instead of shooting, he jammed the butt of his rifle into the snowdrift and began digging around. When the barrel struck the trash can, he paused. "What?" he asked. Then he heard Mittens let out a sound. "What is this?" Connor hit the hard side of the wooden trash can enclosure, then he swept his arm through the accumulated snow on top of it and yanked open the lid. Mittens exploded out of the empty trash can and dashed off toward Sarah. "What the—?" Connor yelled. He aimed his rifle and fired at Mittens. Mittens turned the corner of the alley just seconds before the bullet whizzed and ricocheted against the brick wall.

"Run, girl!" Sarah ordered Mittens when the dog rounded the corner. Sarah threw down her gun and ran to the front of the coffee shop, snatched open the front door, and on lightning-fast legs, she stormed toward her office. As she did, the back door burst open. Connor appeared with his rifle, prepared to fire.

"Time to die!" Connor yelled and fired at Sarah.

Sarah dived into her office and kicked the door closed. "Hurry," she said to herself, crawling to her knocked-over desk.

"There's no escape," Connor yelled again. He kicked the back door shut and walked over to the office door. "I'm going to make you suffer for every word you spoke against my mother, cop. Oh yeah, you're going to suffer real bad." Connor raised his rifle and fired two shots through the office door.

Sarah ducked down as the shots went wide and pinged harmlessly into the tough, thick wood of her old desk. She snatched open the right drawer of her desk and pulled out a revolver. The gun was old but functional and given to her as a present from Pete. Sarah quickly checked the chamber, saw six bullets ready for use, and nodded. "Sometimes old tools are the best," she said just as Connor kicked open the office door to check if his bullets had hit their intended target.

Connor spotted Sarah crouching behind the desk on the floor. He sneered, realizing she was pinned with no escape. He lifted the rifle and aimed it right at her chest. "Die, snowman!" Sarah yelled and squeezed the trigger on the revolver. The gun exploded with deafening sound. Bullets burst through the air. Each bullet struck Connor in his chest and threw him back out into the kitchen. When the chamber emptied out, Sarah slowly crawled to the office door and spotted Connor lying on his back...silent and not moving. His rifle was resting right beside him. "Careful," she whispered and cautiously moved out of her office and went to Connor, expecting the man to jump up at her at any second, despite his wounds. Sarah found a dead body instead – a dead man with six holes in his chest.

"It's finally...over..." Sarah whispered and kicked Connor's rifle away from his hand and then slid down onto the floor and covered her face. The hideous snowman appeared before her eyes with a vicious grin on his face. *You can't kill me, Sarah...I'll always come back in one form or another...you can never kill me.* "Maybe not,"

Sarah said, "but I can save my girl." Sarah opened her eyes, looked around the kitchen, and then grabbed Connor's rifle. "One more snowman to take care of," she said, ran into the front room and then exploded out into the storm. Mittens was waiting for her. "Let's go, girl!" she yelled over the icy winds and heavy snow and began fighting her way down the street. As she did, a loud bang followed by a bright flash came from the police station. Sarah stopped fighting her way through the deep snow. "The trip wire," she said. "Come on, Mittens, we have to hurry!"

While Sarah got her legs moving through the deep snow again, Amanda crashed down onto an icy floor, fighting for her life, as heavy green smoke began to fill the air. "I'm going to kill you!" Robbie yelled, reaching for Amanda's throat. Amanda, coughing from the smoke spewing out of the grenade, managed to fight Robbie's hands away.

"Get off of me!" Amanda yelled and began clawing at Robbie's eyes. Robbie grabbed Amanda's hands and shoved them away from his face.

"I'm not going back to prison!" Robbie yelled and managed to wrap his right hand around Amanda's throat while holding down her left arm. Amanda began choking. She threw her right hand across the floorboards, struggling to find anything that might serve as a weapon. "I'm not going back to prison!" Robbie yelled again and increased pressure on Amanda's throat.

Feeling panic overwhelm her mind, Amanda continued to scrabble around, her body growing weaker by the second. Her hands kept coming up bare. The image of her husband and son flashed through her mind. "Good...bye," she managed to whisper, her world turning dark. But just before she lost consciousness, a loud shot rang out. Her attacker's body was thrown to the side in a heap, as if someone had tossed him away like an old rag. Amanda coughed, grabbed her throat, and then managed to raise her head. She spotted Sarah standing in the shattered doorway, holding Connor's rifle. "What...took you...so long...love?" she asked.

Sarah ran to Amanda, dropped to her knees, and pulled her best friend's head up onto her lap. "Are you okay, June Bug?"

Amanda rubbed her throat. "Your trap...didn't work for one monster but caught another," Amanda replied. She looked over at Robbie's dead body. Snow howling in from the shattered door was slowly beginning to cover it. "Is he dead?"

"How can he not be?" Sarah asked and dropped Connor's rifle. "Firing this rifle nearly broke my shoulder." Sarah locked her eyes on Robbie's chest and saw that he was no longer breathing. *I'll be back, Sarah...I'll always be back...*the snowman hissed and slithered away. "Come on, honey, let's go find Conrad and Andrew."

Amanda grabbed Sarah's hand. "How did you kill Connor?" she begged. "I mean, he's dead...right?"

"Yes, honey, he's dead...thanks to Pete." Sarah let out a heavy breath and allowed the icy wind to cool her face. Even though the winds were cruel and punishing, she cherished the moment. "Think smart...be smart," she whispered and then called out for Mittens. "Mittens, come on, girl!" Mittens ran through the shattered front door, hurried over to Sarah, and began licking her face. "My hero," Sarah smiled and kissed Mittens on her nose. Mittens let out a loud, happy bark and then began licking Amanda.

"I love you, too," Amanda said and felt a relieved smile come over her. "You know something, love?"

"What?"

"If my hubby ever tries to make me leave Snow Falls, I'll punch him square in the nose," Amanda laughed. "I think we've earned our right to call this town home. Besides," Amanda added and crawled up onto her knees, "who cares how much trouble we get into? As long as we have heart and keep up the good fight...who can stop us?"

Sarah smiled, hugged Amanda, and helped her friend stand up. "Let's stay out of trouble for a while," she said, "and focus on the good life. Instead of fighting monsters, how about we go to O'Mally's first thing in the morning and do a little shopping?"

"You bet," Amanda agreed. She took Sarah's hand and walked her back to the lock-up area where they found Conrad and Andrew handcuffed and gagged. Andrew bowed his head with a pained but relieved expression when they walked in. Conrad didn't do much better. "Sometimes a woman has to save the day," Sarah whispered in Amanda's ear and then let out a sweet giggle.

Pete was shocked to see Sarah walk through his office door. "Kiddo!" he exclaimed, jumping to his feet and embracing Sarah.

Sarah wrapped her arms around Pete and hugged him as tight as she could. "Oh, it's so good to see you," she said, taking in a deep breath of coffee, cigar smoke and Chinese noodles. "Your office still smells the same."

"What in the world are you doing here?" Pete asked Sarah and hurried over to clear off a chair for her to sit in. "Don't answer...just let me look at you." Pete took in the pretty pink dress Sarah was wearing. "Pretty as ever," he smiled. "And hey, I like that ponytail."

Sarah blushed. "Oh, Pete," she said and threw her right hand at him, "you always did make me blush."

Pete smiled and plopped down on the edge of his desk. He looked tired, Sarah noticed. His brown suit was wrinkled, and his eyes had dark circles from lack of sleep. "So what brings you back home? Did you decide to take your job back?" he asked in a hopeful voice.

"I've decided," Sarah explained, "to show my love for you, Pete." Sarah reached out and took Pete's hand. "You really saved my can, partner. Connor Barker nearly killed me and everyone I love. Because of you, however, we're all alive."

"All I did was—"

"Be there for me when I needed you," Sarah spoke in a loving voice. "Now I'm going to be here for you." Sarah pointed at Pete's messy desk. "Conrad and Amanda are out having lunch with Amanda's husband. Unfortunately, you and I don't have time for lunch."

Pete looked at his desk and then studied Sarah's eyes. "Boy is that the best news I've heard in months...I'm stuck real hard on this case, kiddo," he said and hurried behind his desk, sat down, and snatched up a brown file. "There's been another robbery and I'm not getting anywhere. Here, take a look."

Sarah took the brown file from Pete. "Pete," she said, "before we start this case...there is something I want you to know."

"What's that, kiddo?" Pete asked, feeling like the old days were finally returning. He grabbed a cigar and shoved it in his mouth, grinning at her.

"Pete, Snow Falls is my home...but Los Angeles will always be my home, too," Sarah said and set the brown file down onto her lap. "I miss you like crazy and I hate being away from you."

"I miss you, too, kiddo," Pete promised.

Sarah felt a tear sting her eye. "I can't stand being away from you...so I've come to offer you a deal."

"A deal?" Pete asked. He leaned forward in his desk chair. "What kind of deal, kiddo?"

"We'll work on your case together, just like the old days, and after we solve it...you retire—"

"Retire?" Pete asked. "Kiddo—"

"Let me finish, you old grouch," Sarah said. "I want us to begin a detective agency, Pete," she explained. "You'll run the agency and every time you get a case I'll fly down to Los Angeles and work on it with you...just like the old days. We'll have a middle ground to work on together. You won't have to work so hard, and we'll get to work together again. Best of all, I won't feel so torn between the two places I love."

Pete leaned back in his chair, chewed on his cigar, and stared at Sarah. "You're serious, aren't you?"

"I can't run from the snowman forever, Pete," Sarah explained. "I miss you, Pete...I miss the life I had in Los Angeles, but I can't give up the life I am building with my husband in Alaska. After I killed Connor Barker, I realized that a part of me can never stop being a cop. Oh, I love being a writer...but if I stop being a cop, the snowman will win. I tried to stop being a cop...and trouble still followed me, Pete. It followed me right up to Alaska and it wouldn't let me go, no matter what." Sarah bit her lip. "Does any of this make sense to you?"

Pete grew very silent and then said: "How much money is this detective agency going to cost me?"

Tears of happiness began falling from Sarah's eyes. She jumped up, ran around Pete's desk, and hugged him. "I'll cover all the expenses, you just be the brains."

Pete wrapped his arms around Sarah and hugged her tight. "Now, now, no tears," he said, struggling to fight back his own, "we have a case to solve, remember?"

"A case...right," Sarah said and walked back to her seat. "So where are we at, Pete?" she asked without wiping her tears away. The tears felt cleansing. Sure, the snowman was still outside in the world somewhere, and sure the nightmares would still come, but Sarah knew that the detective agency work would give her the strength to fight and to balance both parts of her life.

"Well," Pete said, watching Sarah's tears fall, "a rich house up in the canyon was hit," he explained and pointed at the file Sarah was holding. "The thugs took a lot of jewelry and some paintings...the usual." Pete grabbed a file of his own and opened it. "Forensics isn't getting anywhere," he continued to talk. Sarah opened her file and listened to Pete give an official report. As Pete talked, Alaska slowly faded away and the life Sarah once lived in Los Angeles slowly began to wake up. The feeling felt warm and overwhelming – even exciting. It was time to get to work and start mending the past while building the future that her heart deserved to have. A future filled with excitement and perhaps even a few deadly snowmen...but a future surrounded by the people she loved and adored.

"No prints yet?" Sarah asked, focusing on the case. Pete shook his head and continued to fill Sarah in. As he did, a corrupt cop walked past his office door, listened in on the conversation, and slithered away.

ABOUT WENDY

Wendy Meadows is the USA Today bestselling author of many novels and novellas, from cozy mysteries to clean, sweet romances. Check out her popular cozy mystery series Sweetfern Harbor, Alaska Cozy and Sweet Peach Bakery, just to name a few.

If you enjoyed this book, please take a few minutes to leave a review. Authors truly appreciate this, and it helps other readers decide if the book might be for them. Thank you!

Get in touch with Wendy
www.wendymeadows.com

- amazon.com/author/wendymeadows
- goodreads.com/wendymeadows
- bookbub.com/authors/wendy-meadows
- facebook.com/AuthorWendyMeadows
- twitter.com/wmeadowscozy

CPSIA information can be obtained
at www.ICGtesting.com
Printed in the USA
BVHW041519081220
595179BV00012B/1225

9 798560 582715